D1706425

MARRYING OFF HIS BROTHER

MAIL ORDER BRIDES OF CULVER'S CREEK

SUSANNAH CALLOWAY

Tica House
Publishing

Sweet Romance that Delights and Enchants!

Copyright © 2023 by Tica House Publishing LLC

All rights reserved.

No part of this book may be reproduced in any form or by any electronic or mechanical means, including information storage and retrieval systems, without written permission from the author, except for the use of brief quotations in a book review.

PERSONAL WORD FROM THE AUTHOR

Dearest Readers,

Thank you so much for choosing one of my books. I am proud to be a part of the team of writers at Tica House Publishing who work joyfully to bring you stories of hope, faith, courage, and love. Your kind words and loving readership are deeply appreciated.

I would like to personally invite you to sign up for updates and to become part of our **Exclusive Reader Club**—it's completely Free to join! We'd love to welcome you!

Much love,

Susannah Calloway

VISIT HERE to Join our Reader's Club and to Receive Tica House Updates!

https://wesrom.subscribemenow.com/

CONTENTS

CHAPTER 1

Accepting a glass of champagne from a hovering servant, Abigail leaned toward her best friend, Lily, to whisper, "I'm ever so bored. Aren't you?"

Lily subtly nodded behind her own flute. "That officious James Chalmers has no idea how to throw a party."

"No personable young men to meet," Abigail agreed. "Only old matrons, most of them in tawdry black, and fellows his age. Goodness gracious, how are we to meet eligible bachelors?"

"We can't if this is the entirety of our social lives," Lily commented. "Why our fathers dragged us to this dismal affair is quite beyond me."

"Perhaps they want us staying away from the handsome young bucks who'd be tempted to flirt with us." Abigail sipped her champagne. "As though they want us to stay spinsters all our lives."

"What a horrible thought, Abby," Lily chided her. "We must marry. I mean, for pity's sake, we're both twenty years old. In a year or two we'll be too old for any man to want us as wives."

Abigail tapped her finger to her cheek, watching her father, Henry Warner, speak earnestly with their host, James Chalmers. "What do you think they're talking about?"

"Business," Lily replied. "What else do men discuss? Certainly not important topics such as Mrs. Broward's hideously low bodice."

Caught in a fit of laughter, Abigail tried to smother her giggles before they caught the disapproving attention of the horrid Mrs. Broward and her gaggle of cronies. "Oh, my, and the color of her gown. I thought only those unmentionable ladies were allowed to wear such a dark red shade."

"It matches her eyes."

Forced to turn away and hold tightly onto her drink, Abigail coughed her laughter into her fist. "Lily! Stop it. You're so naughty."

"If she had something to *fill* that bodice," Lily went on, her tone dry, "then it might actually be attractive on her."

"I couldn't wear that color," Abigail commented, eyeing Mrs. Broward sidelong. "Even if I filled the bodice."

"No," Lily answered thoughtfully. "Your strawberry hair would clash. As would your green eyes. Warm lavender would suit you the best."

Abigail glanced down at the soft pink gown sewn with white ruffles and trimmed in gold with a critical eye. "I shouldn't wear pink either."

"Didn't you decide on wearing it in order to offend the biddies?"

Abigail choked on her small sip of champagne. "Well, yes. I suppose so."

"It's working as we're both catching looks from old lady Broward and her friends."

Snorting laughter, Abigail did indeed see Old Mrs. Broward watching them with a cold, calculating expression across her seamed face. Two of her friends bent their heads close together, whispering, their beady, narrow gazes on Abigail and Lily.

"They're probably planning an excommunication from the church," Abigail observed.

"Ladies," exclaimed a male voice, startling Abigail and forcing both of them to turn. Their host, James Chalmers, beamed down at them from his tall height. *He looks like a stork.* "I'm so glad you accepted my invitation."

"Thank you, Mr. Chalmers," Abigail said politely. "It's a nice party."

"Yes, yes, a small gathering of my friends."

Abigail didn't like James Chalmers. She never had since the day Henry became his business partner. Now, she really didn't care for the way his chilling eyes roamed up and down her slender frame, hovering over her bosom. She craved to throw her drink in his face in outrage, but suspected that action would bring the wrath of the biddies, and her father, upon her.

"How lovely you look this evening, Abigail," he gushed, taking her hand to bow over it.

Abigail shuddered as he kissed her knuckles. "Thank you."

"I apologize, but I must see to my guests." James winked, then strode quickly away.

Abigail discreetly wiped her hand on her gown. "He didn't even look at you."

"Thank God for that."

"Why?" Abigail took in Lily's bright blonde hair done up in ringlets and falling to her graceful neck. "You're far prettier than I am."

7

Her clear blue eyes troubled, Lily murmured, "We're equally wealthy from good families. So why didn't he flirt with me?"

"Maybe it doesn't matter," Abigail decided. "James is a conniving blackguard. He's as old as our fathers, and believes himself the best thing to ever happen to a woman."

"How do you know that?"

"I spoke with Mrs. Alders not long ago," Abigail replied. "He was interested in her daughter. Courted her for about a month. Mrs. Alders said he never truly conversed with her daughter, he spoke endlessly about himself. Mrs. Alders discovered something about him and ended the courtship immediately."

Lily's eyes widened. "What did she find out?"

"She refused to tell me. But she said, quite firmly, that she'd rather her daughter stay single all her days than marry a man with so few morals."

"What if she's wrong about him?"

Abigail shook her head. "I don't think she is. She wasn't just angry, Lily, she was scared. Frightened silly."

"Oh, that's not good."

"No. It's not. And you know Mrs. Alders to be a kind, sensible woman. Not given to hysterics or vague rumors. She's intelligent with a sharp wit, even if her daughter is a bit simple."

"I've met them both," Lily admitted. "The girl may be soft in her head, but she's kindness itself."

"I think a man like Chalmers would truly hurt a young girl like that."

"You mustn't say that," Lily hissed, glancing around for eavesdroppers. "You can get into trouble."

"It's true, isn't it? Look at him, Lily. Can you see him as a kind, considerate and loving husband?"

"No. He has snake eyes."

"Snake eyes?"

"Of course." Lily frowned. "Haven't you looked into a snake's face? Cold, lidless eyes, no emotion at all."

Abigail grinned. "And how often have *you* looked into a serpent's eyes?"

"Plenty." Lily sniffed. "I'm not afraid of them and have picked them up when I was young and silly. Most snakes are harmless."

"That one over there isn't so harmless," Abigail observed. "Rumors, unconfirmed mind you, have said Chalmers didn't create his wealth through honest means. That all this." Abigail waved her hand at the extravagant ballroom in the Chalmers mansion. "Came from someone else's blood."

"As in?" Lily's blue eyes all but fell from their sockets.

"You know what I'm talking about. Don't make me say it."

"Maybe that's what Mrs. Alders discovered about him. And that it's not just unconfirmed rumors."

"That occurred to me, too."

"You don't suppose your father," Lily began, reluctant, "also made his fortune in a, er, bad way?"

Abigail studied her tall, handsome, smiling father as he talked with an elderly male guest. "Most came from honest means," she replied slowly. "He made a few very smart investments. His money grew at a fascinating rate once he and James got together."

"Does that frighten you?"

Abigail smiled tightly. "Very much."

Unable to stop thinking of the previous evening's conversation with Lily, Abigail studied Henry covertly at the breakfast table. He read the Boston paper as he forked eggs into his mouth, followed by a gulp of coffee. While Abigail respected her father, she wondered what had happened to the love they were supposed to have for one another.

Raised by a succession of nannies since her mother died, Abigail never had a chance to be close to Henry. He treated her with a vague sort of indifference, as though she was a stray cat the servants adopted. Dining on her own fried potatoes, bacon, scrambled eggs, and bread, Abigail considered the hugs she'd never received, the praise he'd never offered, the love he seemed incapable of giving.

"Father," she asked, forcing him to lower his paper with a frown, "how did you get so rich?"

Henry's frown deepened. "Intelligent investments and excellent business dealings. Why?"

"Why are you partners with Mr. Chalmers?"

He lowered the paper. "Why are you so interested?"

"Because he's not a nice man."

"One doesn't have to be nice to be successful." Henry snorted. "And he's very successful. Being nice can have the opposite effect, you know."

"So you don't mind your name being associated with a man like him?"

"Of course not," Henry snapped. "James is a very astute businessman. Everyone knows it. He's friends with the mayor, plans to enter politics himself in the coming years. And it's not such a bad idea for you to cultivate a pleasant relationship with him."

Abigail narrowed her eyes. "Why? I don't care for him."

"Because I'm entering into new negotiations with him," Henry answered impatiently. Plans that might increase our partnership and take it to different levels."

"That doesn't concern me."

"So, what does?"

"That my name is associated with that of a monster."

Henry picked his paper up to rattle it with finality. "You'd best change your mind about James. He's becoming a very important factor in our lives."

In the afternoon perhaps three days later, Abigail sat at her secretary, writing letters to various relatives and friends. She carefully penned each one with meticulous script, her handwriting as perfect as she could make it. A maid, Millicent, stood nearby to fetch her mistress tea, or run an errand. As Abigail folded each letter with meticulous care and added them to their envelopes, she then stacked them in a tidy pile.

"Miss Warner?"

Abigail glanced up to find the head housekeeper, Caroline, standing in the doorway. "Yes?"

"Your father wishes to speak with you, ma'am. He's in his study."

"He's home? At this time of day?"

"Yes, ma'am."

Abigail stood, then picked up the stack to hand to Millicent. "Please take these to the post office."

"Yes, ma'am."

Wondering what had brought Henry home so early in the afternoon, Abigail glided past the servants to make her way down the long hallway. Henry's study was also the family library, a big room just opposite the vast, formal drawing room. As her father decreed had decreed that no one entered without knocking first, Abigail knocked on the closed door.

"Come."

Henry sat behind his wide mahogany desk, books stacked upon shelves on all the walls around him. The shelves rose from the floor to the tall ceiling with ladders to navigate those at the top. The afternoon sunlight streamed in through the windows, the curtains drawn back.

"You wanted to see me?"

Henry glanced up from his papers. "Yes, sit down. We have an important matter to discuss."

She sat gingerly on one of the plush chairs. "And what would that be?"

"Your marriage."

Abigail froze, ice flowing through her veins as her body drew cold, then even colder. "I'm to be married?"

"Indeed, yes." Henry eyed the papers before him. "I'm looking at the marriage contract. It seems to be in order."

"And do I know my prospective husband?" Abigail bit her lip, her stomach churning in distress. *I should have known this was coming. He'll marry me to an associate, someone he needs to advance his wealth and prestige. Please, let him be a decent man, a gentleman whom I may fall in love with.*

"Of course." Henry frowned. "James and I have been discussing this for weeks. He's made a handsome offer for your hand. After some negotiations, we've come to an agreement."

"J-James? As in Chalmers?"

"Well, yes. Of course James Chalmers. Who else would it be?"

Abigail felt sick. Sick as though she'd need to run to the nearest basin and throw up. *No, no, he can't do this to me. I'm his daughter, he must know what James is truly like. What he's done.* Her body, her face, burned as though she'd come down with a terrible fever.

"Daughter? You should be pleased with this arrangement. James will one day be governor, mark my words. You can do far worse than he as your husband. No other man in Boston has his connections, his business acumen."

Her hands clenched into fists in her lap, Abigail found some semblance of courage. Of defiance. "No."

"No? No what?"

She raised her eyes. "No. I won't marry him. Nor can you force me to."

Henry, his face tight, his eyes deadly serious, leaned over his desk. "I *can* force you. I *will* force you. You marriage to James will come in one month. Be ready."

CHAPTER 2

"Where the hell have you been?"

Mitch gazed down at his elder brother, Silas, in surprise. "Fixing the fences in the north pasture. What's gotten you twisted into a knot?"

Silas blew out a harsh bark. "You doing the work I need you to? That's a laugh."

Reining in the sharp anger that surged to heat his face, Mitch slowly dismounted his gelding. He faced Silas while fighting to prevent a loud outburst of shouted insults. "Yeah. This ranch is also mine."

"Pa left it to me because you're lazier than a bear in hibernation."

Mitch sucked in a deep breath. "Then if I have no stake in it, I've no reason to stick around. Right? Leave you to run it yourself."

Something flickered in Silas's deep blue eyes. "You have nowhere to go."

Mitch shrugged. "A ranch hand with a good horse can get work anywhere."

"Except you *don't* work," Silas snapped. "You ride that nag all over without doing a lick of anything useful."

Turning his back, Mitch led the tired bay into the barn. Nearly every day, it seemed, he'd had the same argument with Silas since their father's funeral the year before. Silas demanding, haranguing, accusing Mitch of not helping enough with the ranch chores. He fully expected Silas to follow him, continue his tirade, warn Mitch of what could happen if he didn't pull his share of the load.

Out of the icy winter chill, Mitch unsaddled his tall bay, curried the damp mahogany hide. In here, the body warmth of the stabled horses, the milk cow, and her calf, prevented the biting November cold to affect him much. The barn cats, able mousers, rubbed against his boots. With the coming of the dusk, the chickens flapped their way to the rafters for their safe night's sleep.

"Where would I go if I left here?" he murmured as he led the bay into his stall. "I've always had a hankering to see Colorado. The mountains. Pack up and just go."

Mitch pondered his options as he fed the horses and milked the patient cow. The cats meowed for their share, lapping the sweet milk from the pan he set down for them. Carrying the bucket, he let himself out into the bitter wind, and shut the door behind him.

The ranch house's lights were lit from within, the scent of woodsmoke drifting to his nostrils as he crossed the yard. He also detected the odors of snow and ice on the brisk breeze. *Storm coming. Be here by this time tomorrow.* He let himself into the warm, brightly lit kitchen, and set the milk bucket on the counter.

His widowed mother, Maryanne, smiled from the stove as he doffed his hat and heavy coat to hang on pegs. "You're just in time. Wash up, honey."

Silas's wife, Gillian, busily set the long wooden table. "What happened between you and Silas? He's madder than a rabid dog."

Washing his hands at the sink, Mitch shrugged. "He always mad anymore. Nothing I do is right, or good enough."

Drying them, he met his mother's concerned gaze. "Maybe it's time I packed up. Left. Start my own place."

Both women stopped, frozen in place at this suggestion. "Mitch, don't say that," Maryanne pleaded. "We need you here."

"That's not how I see it." Mitch leaned against the counter. "I have no claim to this ranch, or anything on it. Silas saw to that. Pa didn't include me in his will."

"That's not true –" Maryanne started to say, then caught sight of Silas entering the kitchen. "Silas, tell Mitch he's wanted and needed here. Your father set up something up for him. Yes?"

Silas slid into a chair, his expression neutral. "Pa gave a portion of land to Mitch."

Astounded, Mitch glared. "And why wasn't I told this? You kept this from me all this time?"

"Yep. Sure did."

His rage rising, Mitch straightened. "Why?"

"Pa's plan, little brother. He knew you were likely to run that land as shoddy as you do the rest of it. He put in a stipulation that you don't receive anything until you settle down with a wife."

"You're lying!"

"Nope. I'm not." Silas met his hot gaze without flinching. "Rachel Moore is quite the catch. She'd make you a very fine wife."

Mitch bared his teeth in a humorless grin. "I happen to dislike Rachel, big brother. She's spoiled, mean spirited, and not the catch you seem to think she is."

"I think she'd –"

Maryanne got no further. Silas banged his fist on the table, making the crockery jump. "You don't have a choice, Mitch," he snapped. "She's the only eligible lady within a hundred miles. Marry her, and you have land, and an income of your own."

"I won't marry her."

"Then you get nothing."

"Silas, stop it," Maryanne cried. "You're not being fair. You accuse Mitch of laziness, but you sit on your backside and make demands. You're denying your own flesh and blood his inheritance. I won't tolerate it."

"You don't have much choice, Ma," Silas replied coldly. "I'm the sole executor of Pa's will. I make the decisions concerning it."

"Your father would be ashamed of what you're doing," Maryanne snapped. "I'm ashamed of you."

"Don't worry about it, Ma," Mitch said. "Silas, you keep the ranch. Run it by yourself. I'm gone."

Taking his hat from its peg, Mitch set it firmly on his head as both Maryanne and Gillian protested.

"Mitch, no," Gillian called. "Silas, tell him to stay."

"Don't leave, Mitch," Maryanne cried, tears standing in her eyes. "I love you, I need you."

His anger softening a fraction, Mitch kissed her cheek. "Sorry, Ma."

Donning his coat, Mitch let himself out into the cold and the dark, his heart aching in his chest. Through the walls, he heard both Maryanne and Gillian raise their voices as they berated Silas. Knowing his brother wouldn't be deterred by their shouts or tears, he flipped the coat's collar up, and headed for the barn to saddle his horse.

The hour had grown late, and the bitter wind cut through to his bones by the time Mitch rode into the small town of Culver's Creek, Missouri. After paying for a night's stabling at the livery, then a room at the hotel, he crossed the street to walk into the town's single saloon. Greeted by warmth from the stove, laughing voices and piano music, he sat at a small table as close to the stove as he could get.

"Mitchell Ellison," called a familiar voice. "Get yourself over here, you mutt."

Grinning, Mitch rose to wend his way amid the tables filled with ranch hands, gamblers, and a few local men to his friend's table. Freddie Winston shook his hand, also grinning, and gestured toward the empty chair.

"What brings you in here so late?" Freddie asked, lifting his hand to beckon the barmaid.

"My brother." Mitch opened his coat, set his hat on the chair's back. "We had a quarrel."

Freddie's eyes narrowed. "Quarrel over what?"

Mitch knew Freddie didn't miss much. As Culver's Creek's sheriff, Freddie kept a watchful eye on strangers passing through, the current crop of gamblers and rowdy ranch hands spending their hard-earned cash on whiskey. Though only ten years older than Mitch, Freddie looked young, as though he and Mitch were of the same age.

Mitch glanced up as the bar maid approached. "A beer, please."

He caught the speculative glance she sent him before she left the table, her hips swinging in a seductive fashion. Nor did Freddie miss her silent invitation.

"I wouldn't if I were you," Freddie advised, lifting his beer mug. "She's trouble."

Mitch rolled his eyes. "I didn't come to town for that."

"Then what's going on with you? You don't ride three miles in this weather just to pass the time."

"I told you. I had a fight with Silas. I left."

"Silas is a disagreeable sort," Freddie agreed. "Has a high opinion of himself. Course, most sensible folks have a different opinion of him."

"I'm thinking to pack my horse and leave," Mitch commented. "Start somewhere fresh."

"And leave your ma? Don't be so hasty, son. She about fell apart when your pa died. If she loses you, I don't think she'll recover."

"What am I to do?"

Mitch stopped as the barmaid appeared with his beer and yet another sultry glance. He paid for his drink without meeting her gaze, hoping she'd get the non-verbal hint he wasn't interested. She departed with a distinct huff.

Lowering his voice, Mitch went on. "Silas withheld my inheritance. Now says Pa left me land, but I can't get it without marrying first."

Freddie almost choked on his beer. "What? That ain't right. Your pa was a good man, he wouldn't leave you with nothing."

"According to the will's executor, he did."

"I say fight it," Freddie declared. "Get a lawyer, make Silas open the will for all to see."

"Without money to pay that lawyer?" Mitch shook his head. "I don't want to marry, and I sure don't want to marry Rachel Moore."

"Why her?"

"Silas sort of insisted I ask Rachel to marry me."

Freddie tapped his fingers on the table, gazing into empty space. "She's not the right girl for you. Too hot headed, dumb as a stump. I say you should find a suitable lady without Silas's say-so."

"And just where do I find a suitable lady?" Mitch demanded. "There are none. This part of Missouri isn't exactly a hub of social interaction. This town is the backwater of all backwaters."

"I never said find a gal in western Missouri." Freddie smirked.

"Oh, that makes so much sense. I should ride to St. Louis, kidnap a gal off the street, and throw her on the back of my saddle. You're brilliant."

"I am, son."

"Uh, huh." Mitch drank his beer while contemplating the lure of Colorado and the Rocky Mountains. *I should just pack up and go. Ma will come to understand in time.*

"The War killed young men by the hundreds of thousands," Freddie continued conversationally. "Both in the North and in the South."

"A history lesson now?"

"Nope. A fact. There are more women in the East needing husbands than ever before. Just as there are men in the west needing wives."

Mitch scowled. "Get to the point."

"Advertise for a Mail Order Bride, son."

"Uh." Mitch shook his head. "That doesn't sound right. Women don't marry strangers."

"It happens all the time. You write a letter stating what you're looking for in a wife, then the Agency matches you with a lady needing a man. Simple."

"And if I don't like her when she gets here?" Mitch shook his head again. "No. I can't do that."

"Just think about it, Mitch. You get to know her a bit. If it doesn't work, then you always have Rachel to fall back on."

Half-drunk, tired, emotionally strung out, Mitch stumbled into his hotel room. He turned the lamp's wick up, then sat on the bed's edge and stared at the floor. "Mail Order Bride, eh? That'd show ole Silas, wouldn't it?"

Still, he couldn't imagine any young woman in her right mind consenting to marry him – a stranger with nothing. No money, no land, few prospects. "How can I bring a nice gal into this miserable place when I have so little to offer her?"

Do it. Once you marry, the land is yours. Silas has no say then.

Spotting paper and a pen on the desk in the room's corner, Mitch took the lamp to it and sat down. "What do I say?"

After staring at the wall for a few long moments, he picked up the pen and started to write.

CHAPTER 3

Abigail sobbed in Lily's arms. "How can he do this to me? I'm his daughter, and he's selling me to Chalmers as though I mean nothing. Nothing at all."

Lily stroked her hair, murmuring shushing sounds. "Stop crying, dear. Stop. We'll figure something out. Right? There has to be a solution. We'll just have to find it."

Wiping her face, Abigail sat up. "Can I stay here with you?"

Lily smiled. "You know you can. For as long as you want to. My folks already think of you as their daughter."

Hope warmed Abigail's frightened heart. "Really?"

"But your father will find you here," Lily went on, sadly. "He'll drag you to the altar. You did say he'd force you to marry this man. Yes?"

"Yes," Abigail whispered, realizing that Lily's parents couldn't protect her. Not from Henry Warner. Her father. "So what do I do? Where can I go?"

"Marry someone else, Abby."

Abigail blinked. "How do I do that? Just ask some random stranger to marry me?"

"Not quite." Rising, Lily strode to her secretary, and picked up a newspaper. "I saw this just this morning. As we talked, I remembered it."

Returning, Lily handed the paper to Abigail, then pointed to an advert. "Read it."

Abigail read, growing more and more incredulous. "A Mail Order Bride? Is this a joke?"

"No joke." Lily sat beside her, her expression solemn. "In the West, men need wives. There aren't very many young men here in Boston, nor anywhere in the East. Find a husband, my dear. Go away. Far away from your father and Chalmers. They'll never find you."

Rereading the advert, Abigail tried to imagine herself as the wife of a man she hadn't met. "I suppose this can't be worse than marrying Chalmers," she murmured.

Lily rubbed Abigail's back in a loving gesture. "You can go through the letters, choose the man who suits you the most.

Ask for time to know him before the wedding. If he's cruel, you can still walk away."

"But I have only a month," Abigail protested. "Father will marry me to Chalmers when he returns from his trip to New York."

"Then you'd best get busy. Here, I'll help you with your letter."

Weeks passed. Abigail, growing desperate, read and reread every letter she received from men in the western United States. Miners, farmers, businessmen. From territories such as Colorado, New Mexico, Texas, Oklahoma. Even one from as far away as Oregon.

In Lily's room, Abigail sorted through the latest batch. "How do I choose?" she cried, terrified she'd choose the wrong man.

Lily read a letter. "Listen to this: *My name is Mitchell Ellison from Culver's Creek, Missouri. I'm a rancher, and I live with my mother, my brother and sister-in-law. I need a wife. I promise to be a good husband. I work hard, hoping to have my own land one day. I don't know much about women. What I do know scares me. I'm willing to give a lady a good and loving home with kids, and I'll never lift a hand in anger.*

Lily met Abigail's gaze with hope. "He sounds the best of all. Most of these others only want a wife for the free labor. The majority are barely literate. See his hand? He writes well."

Abigail read the missive. "None of the others promised to treat their wife and children kindly," she murmured. "You're right. He sounds educated."

"Wire him immediately." Lily stood and took Abigail's hand. "We'll ask the coachman to take us to the wire office. Then we book you a train ticket, first class, to Missouri."

Treading a fine line with her father, Abigail secretly set her plans in motion. With Lily's help, she emptied her bank account into ready cash, packed only what she couldn't bear to leave behind. A locket with a portrait of her mother. Her mother's Bible. Her mother's wedding ring that Henry placed in a box then forgot about. Abigail took it, hoping for a romantic wedding in which her husband placed the ring on her finger.

"Tomorrow," Lily told her as they sat together in Abigail's chamber, the door closed to prevent the servants from listening or observing. "I'll come by with our coach. Right after your father leaves for his office."

"What about the housekeeper?" Abigail asked. "She'll see my satchel. She'll suspect I'm leaving."

Lily nibbled her lip in thought. "All right, bribe her to keep her silence. Pay her a few dollars to look the other way. By the time your father comes home, finds you gone, she can say she didn't see you leave. She doesn't know what happened to you."

"Caroline is a kindly woman," Abigail agreed. "She's been our housekeeper since before my mother died."

"Then she's loyal. What time does your father leave?"

"Around nine."

"The train leaves at noon." Lily paused. "Yes, that should give us enough time. It may be close, however. I'll instruct our coachman to wait where we can see your door. Once your father leaves, we'll fetch you."

"What in the world would I do without you?" Abigail embraced Lily hard, near tears.

"Marry a fiend." Lily choked on a sob. "I'll miss you so much. Promise to write me."

"I will. Every week."

Lily wiped her tears with her fingers. "If things go bad for you, wire me. I'll get you back here to Boston."

"All right."

Lily smiled. "I know you'll find happiness out there, Abby. This Mitchell Ellison truly sounds like a good man."

"I hope so. This is all so frightening, though. Marrying a stranger in a land called Missouri. His town isn't even on a map."

"It's there. Have faith you're doing the right thing, dear. Because you are."

Abigail squeezed Lily's fingers, trying to smile through her tears. "I'll try. I really will."

"I've sent Millicent on an errand," Caroline said, her voice low. "If she's questioned, she can honestly say she doesn't know anything."

Her stomach fluttering, churning, making her nauseous, Abigail peered around the corner of a wall at the top of the stairs. From here, she and Caroline had an excellent view of the front door.

And Henry's exit from the house.

"Good," Abigail whispered. "What about you?"

"Mr. Warner has little time or patience for servants," Caroline answered. "He'll ask, I'll say I don't know, he'll search for you himself."

Abigail groped for and seized Caroline's hand. "Thank you for helping me."

"I don't agree with his choice of a husband for you, ma'am," Caroline replied. "If I may say so, Mr. Chalmers is a bad man. You've been a kind mistress to work for. Much as your mother was."

"And if my father sacks you?"

Caroline shrugged with a small smile. "A good housekeeper can always find work."

"Shh," Abigail hissed, backing into hiding. "There he is."

Henry, briefcase in his hand, paused by the front door to don his hat, gloves and long black coat. Outside, Boston's frigid wind had brought a storm of snow and sleet the night before. Holding her breath, Abigail watched as he buttoned his coat, then departed the house.

She sucked in a sharp gust of breath. "Oh, my. I don't think my nerves can handle much more."

"Let's get you warmly wrapped for the journey, ma'am."

A short while later, garbed in boots, heavy coat, scarves, and a wool cloak, Abigail waddled down the stairs. Caroline followed with her satchel and set it beside the door. She smiled as she patted Abigail's swathed cheek.

"May God bless and keep you, ma'am."

"And you. Take care of yourself, Caroline."

Lily's carriage stood outside her door, drawn by a pair of black horses. The driver tipped his cap to her, and took her satchel in hand. Lily waved from the coach's rear as the driver set her satchel in the rear. He then assisted her inside the big carriage. Abigail glanced at her home, the only home she'd ever known, as Caroline dipped her chin in a brief nod, then closed the door.

Lily was already weeping. "I'm going to miss you so much."

Abigail held her, also crying, her tears dripping into her wool scarf. "Don't weep. We're supposed to be happy. I'm going to be wed."

That assurance failed. Abigail and Lily hugged, wept, and talked through their tears the entire journey to the train station. Once there, the driver handed her down, and set her satchel outside an office. An employee inspected her ticket, summoned a porter.

"Follow him, ma'am, he'll take you to your train."

Helpless, hoping for one last embrace, Abigail stared wildly at Lily who still sat in the coach's shelter.

"Goodbye, my dear," Lily sobbed, her cheek red from cold and crying. "I love you."

"I love you, too."

The driver snapped his whip over the team, and Lily vanished into the crowded Boston traffic of horses and carriages, and mules and wagons. Turning, Abigail rushed after the porter, trying not to slip on the slick platform. Many trains huffed on the myriad of tracks, and her porter darted around several before halting at a locomotive in what seemed like the station's center.

Abigail, breathing hard, tipped him a dollar, then showed her ticket to the conductor. He bowed, then escorted her to her first-class berth, explaining where the meal car was, what hours meals were served, and if she had any need at all, she was to ask for him personally.

"Thank you," Abigail said weakly, examining the small cabin where she'd spend most of her time while traveling to Mitchell and Missouri.

Comfortable looking, it had a narrow bunk, an armchair, a sink, fluffy towels and a large window where she might sit and watch the country pass by. For the first time, she felt a thrill of excitement. She'd never traveled outside Boston before. Now she'd cross many states to the man whom she'd promised to marry.

"Please be a good man, Mitchell," she murmured, sitting on her bunk. "Please be kind, generous, and a loving husband. I vow to be a good and loving wife, to raise our children to also be kind and loving. Please, let us be happy together."

Despite the many comforts her first class ticket brought her, Abigail arrived in the tiny, ugly, dismal town of Culver's Creek, Missouri exhausted and irritable. Rain and snow had turned the dirt streets to mud. Only a smattering of people walked along the main avenue through town. Horses and mules trotted through the muck, splashing nastiness everywhere.

She stared at the lack of anything resembling civilization in dismay.

And fear.

"What have I done?"

The porter set her satchel beside her, then dashed away before she could tip him. Bitterly cold, the stiff breeze chilling her to the bone, Abigail swiped tendrils of her hair from her face as she gazed around for her bridegroom.

Mitchell had described himself as tall, with ash blond hair, blue eyes. No one stepped toward her or seemed to look for her. The small gaggle of folks who'd arrived for the mail scattered as they left the station. Her fear struck her afresh. *What if Mitchell changed his mind? What if he isn't coming for me?*

She flexed her cold fingers in her gloves, fighting panic. Alone, in a strange town, among strangers, Abigail had nowhere to turn. Did this dismal place have a hotel? Perhaps a boarding house? What was she to do?

"Miss Warner?"

Her heart in her throat, Abigail spun around.

Before her stood the most attractive man she thought she'd ever seen. None of the young bucks in Boston compared to the tall young man who whipped his cowboy hat from his head. Thick, dark blond hair curled over his brow, around his neck. His broad shoulders spoke of hard work and solid masculinity. Blue eyes that pierced her through met hers. And the kindest, brightest smile that illuminated the dreary daylight smiled at her.

"I'm Mitch Ellison," he said, taking her hand. "Welcome to Culver's Creek."

CHAPTER 4

Mitch scarcely believed what his eyes told him. The tiny woman wrapped up in coats and scarves and a wool shawl peeped up at him with eyes of the purest green. Her pale red hair, somewhat disheveled under the brisk wind, was a shade he'd never encountered before. Her porcelain skin made him think of fine China, and her amazingly high cheekbones made him suddenly crave to run his fingers over them.

Her lush, full lips smiled, though they trembled slightly. "I'm Abigail Warner. A pleasure, I'm sure."

Mitch barely felt the cold snow under his boots. Her accent both delighted and fascinated him. He imagined her body under all the wraps was so slender he could place his hands on her waist and his fingers would meet. "I, um, the buggy's this way. Is this your bag?"

"Yes, it is."

Hardly able to take his gaze from her, Mitch donned his hat. "This way, ma'am."

Abigail strode at his side as he led the way across the platform, and when her boots slipped, he seized her arm above the elbow. "Careful there. We've had a bit of sleet recently."

Recovering, she glanced up at him with gratitude and a smile. "Thank you."

After hefting the satchel into the buggy, he helped her up to the seat. "It's cold, ma'am, so I brought a fur for you."

"That's very kind of you, Mr. Ellison."

"Mitch." He grinned. "We're not very formal around here."

After he climbed up, he tucked the warm bear fur around her waist and legs, and even under her boots. "It's a long way to the ranch."

"How far is a long way?"

"About four miles. It'll take us about an hour to get there, maybe a tad more."

Taking the reins, Mitch clucked to the gray gelding, who started off at a brisk trot. From the corner of his eye, he saw Abigail looking at the town of Culver's Creek that passed them by.

"Not much of a town," he commented. "But folks are nice for the most part. Good people. Honest, hardworking."

"It's smaller than I'd anticipated," Abigail admitted.

"Now the railroad's come through," he said, "it'll grow. Though I'm not sure if that's a good thing. What's Boston like?"

"Big," she answered. "Noisy. Traffic through every street. But it has restaurants, hotels, art museums, theaters. Any night of the week, you can see a play."

"Yeah?" Mitch grinned. "Around here, the only thing that play are the cats, calves and colts."

Abigail chuckled. "What's your family like?"

"Oh, you'll love my ma. She's got the biggest heart. Gillian, my sister-in-law, well, she's kind and sweet. A great cook. Wants kids so bad."

"And your brother?"

Mitch's smile faded. "We don't always get along, I'll warn you now. We tend to quarrel. Maybe too much. But don't let that trouble you."

"I'll do my best."

Mitch eyed her sidelong. "And you? Do you think you can be happy here?"

Abigail turned her face to gaze at the snow and brown grass, the simple track that led to his family's home. "I hope so," she said simply. "I hope we can find happiness together. With one another. Have a family."

"I won't rush you," Mitch said quickly. "Let's take a month to get to know one another. You live with us in the guest room, learn what we're all about. And if you don't like it, me, I'll help you onto a train to either home, or wherever you want to go. Is that a fair deal?"

Her brilliant smile quite took his breath away. "More than fair."

"Uh, good." Mitch all but strangled over his words. "Great."

Mitch watched her face carefully, discreetly, as the gray gelding trotted into the wide yard. He tried seeing his home through her eyes – the big barn, the sheds, the chickens scratching amid the weeds and gravel, the corral with horses munching hay, the smokehouse. Abigail stared at the sprawling ranch house made of timber and river stone, the chimney puffing blue smoke, the wide veranda.

He also noticed the flicker of disappointment that crossed her lovely face and was gone.

"This is your home?" Abigail asked, taking everything in.

"It may not be what you're used to," he said, lame.

He reined the gray in at the veranda. Maryanne and Gillian, shawls over their shoulders, stepped from the house to gape as Mitch handed Abigail down from the buggy. Under their confused stares, he slid his arm through hers, and guided her up the steps.

"Ma," he began, his tone formal, "this is Abigail Warner. She's my fiancé."

Maryanne, her mouth trembling, reached for Abigail and took her hands. "My dear girl, come inside, quickly. You're so cold you're blue. This is Gillian. Mitch, see to that horse then come inside. You've got some explaining to do."

Abigail sent him a frightened glance over her shoulder as Maryanne and Gillian hustled her into the house and shut the door.

After caring for the horse, Abigail's satchel in his hand, Mitch crossed the yard to the house. He saw no sign of Silas, yet Silas's stocky black gelding stood in the corral. Upon opening the kitchen door, he doffed his hat – and grinned before he'd hung his hat on the peg.

"I reckon you know how we found one another."

A cup of steaming tea in her hands, her wraps and coats off, Abigail stunned him with her simple beauty. She sat at the table, smiling, as Maryanne and Gillian sat with her, beaming with joy.

"A real Mail Order Bride," Gillian said, her tone admiring. "That's so brave of you, dear. To come all this way to marry a stranger."

"And she chose my boy." Maryanne smiled. "I'm so blessed. We all are. Mitch, why didn't you tell us?"

Because I didn't want Silas to know. "I reckon I wanted it to be a surprise."

"It certainly is," Maryanne marveled. "Abigail, my dear, aren't there eligible young men in Boston?"

"No," she replied, looking down at her tea. "Not really. Most men are already engaged. Or married."

"So you picked our Mitch." Gillian patted her hand, laughing. "Girl, you selected a good one. He's special."

"I wouldn't say that."

Silas paced into the kitchen, his expression, set, neutral. "So this is where you've been all day." He looked Abigail up and down with an air of contempt. "Finding a lady friend instead of repairing the fence. Too bad about our cattle roaming free."

Mitch's grin changed to a scowl instantly. "Silas, this is my fiancé, Abigail Warner, from Boston. Abigail, my brother, Silas."

Silas reached across the table to shake her hand, his smile of welcome brittle. "Nice to meet you, Abby."

"Please." Abigail withdrew her hand. "I'm Abigail. Only one person is allowed to address me as Abby."

"Oh, a big city debutante," Silas commented dryly. "My apologies, Your Majesty."

Abigail shunted her gaze to her tea as Mitch paced forward, his fists clenched. Maryanne, standing, planted her hand on his chest, effectively stopping him.

"Silas, that's uncalled for," Maryanne snapped, outraged. "Abigail is a guest under our roof. Treat her as such or sleep in the barn."

He cocked his eyes at Maryanne. "Not much of a choice, Ma," he said dryly.

Turning, he departed the way he'd come.

Her body stiff, Abigail thrust Gillian's comforting hand from her arm. "I'm quite all right, thank you."

"I'm so sorry," Maryanne said, sitting again. "Silas, he hasn't been himself since his father died. Please forgive his terrible behavior. You're welcome and wanted here."

Abigail nodded without looking up. "Thank you."

Itching to throw Silas into an icy water trough and hold him under, Mitch contained his rage long enough to say, "I'll show you to the guest room, if you'd like."

"I would. Very much."

Abigail walked just behind him as Mitch carried her satchel down the hall to the spacious guest room. He set her bag just inside but did not cross the threshold. "It's fairly comfortable," he told her, subdued. "We've got plenty of blankets, quilts, even the fur to keep you warm. And if there's anything you need, just let us know."

Abigail gazed around at the wide bed with thick blankets, the bureau, the small writing desk and chair. Her smile appeared fragile to him. "I'm sure I'll be fine, thank you."

Mitch craved to hold her tightly against him, hating the haunted look in her huge green eyes. "I'm so sorry about my brother. Please don't let him bother you. As Ma said, he's changed since Pa died last year."

"I'm very tired from the journey," she said. "May I rest for a while?"

"Of course, sure." Mitch didn't care for how she refused to look at him. "Consider yourself at home."

He closed the door behind him, as troubled as Abigail appeared to be.

Returning to the warm kitchen, he sat heavily at the table. "Dammit."

"No swearing," Maryanne admonished him instantly. "Stop worrying about Silas. He'll accept Abigail in time."

"Ma's right," Gillian added, her arm over his shoulders. "You've found a perfectly lovely lady, Mitch. I think she's wonderful. When's the wedding?"

"Once we get to know one another." Mitch found some happiness in his choice of a Mail Order Bride. "I'd say a month. She'll stay in the guest room until then. Is that all right?"

"Don't be silly," Maryanne declared, bustling forward to kiss his brow. "It's simply perfect. You still should have told us about her."

"I know. Sorry about that."

As Maryanne and Gillian prepared a nice ham for supper, talking excitedly about weddings and babies and another member of the family, Mitch listened with half an ear. He worried about Abigail, and the clear animosity Silas displayed toward her.

What's with him? Why isn't he welcoming of her? He wanted me to marry, claimed that's what Pa wanted me to do for me to inherit. Now I am, and he behaves as though I'd asked a painted lady to be my wife.

Nor did the icy atmosphere melt over the delicious dinner of baked ham, mashed potatoes, beans cooked in butter, hot bread, and apple pie for dessert. Silas's acid comments regarding Abigail as a suitable bride angered Mitch until he almost launched himself over the table at Silas's throat.

Abigail never looked up from her meal.

"Can you cook, Abby?" Silas asked. "Mitch can't. He's as helpless and as useless as a kitten. By the way, he doesn't work. You're marrying a lazy, no-account fool of a man. I thought I'd mention it before the ceremony."

"That's enough," Maryanne cried. "Silas, you're excused from the table."

"I'm not done eating."

"Yes." Her glare skewered him where he sat. "You are. Go to your room like the spoiled and misbehaving child you are. And don't think I won't put you over my knee, boy."

His face flushing crimson, Silas slammed his way from the table and from the kitchen. Mitch didn't watch him leave but tried to get Abigail to look at him from sheer willpower alone. Abigail ignored his command, however.

"I'm sorry –" he began.

"*Don't* apologize for him, Mitchell," Maryanne snapped. "He's behaving like a six-year-old child who didn't get what he wanted for his birthday. Silas *will* apologize. Abigail, I promise, he'll mend his ways. If I must spank him every day of the month, he will."

Abigail raised her face with a tight smile. "That's all right. I'm sure he has his reasons."

"He does *not*," Gillian growled. "He's my husband, and I love him, but he's not acting like himself. Abigail, I swear, he's not normally rude like this."

"Thank you all for your kind words," Abigail murmured. "But I don't think I can marry into a situation as bad as this is. I'm sorry, but I'm going to retire for the evening. Good night."

Stunned, Mitch watched her leave the kitchen, her head bowed, her reddish hair falling around her shoulders. He wanted to both hold her in his arms and soothe her troubles and strangle Silas with his bare hands. He did neither.

"Silas turned the best thing I've ever had away from me," he said, his voice a low growl. "He'll damn well pay for it, too."

CHAPTER 5

Abigail slept deeply and well that night. After the train's constant motion, cuddled under the mound of blankets and furs, the door opened to catch the warm air from the stove and hearth, she failed to even dream. Not even sleeping under a strange roof amid strangers troubled her slumber.

Loud and angry voices brought her from the depths.

Grayish sunlight seeped between the curtains as Abigail roused, the air outside her face bitterly cold. She huddled under her covers, craving sleep, rest, and the escape from the memories, and the angry voices. Opening her eyes, she stared at the ceiling, listening even as she wished she couldn't hear them yell about her.

"She's a spoiled rich idiot," Silas shouted. "She's incapable of handling her share of the chores."

"Abigail will learn," Mitch shot back. "What's the matter with you? Why can't you accept her?"

"Because she's useless. Just as you are. Why don't you both run off together and leave me to run this ranch?"

"It's Mitch's ranch, too," Maryanne screeched. "Silas, stop this nonsense right now. He has as much right to this place as you do. Now he's found a wife, just as you wanted, and you're angrier than a badger with a tooth ache. Why?"

"Never mind," Silas snapped. "If he wants to marry a useless fool, then let him. He and she better pull their shares of the load. Or they're both off this property."

Abigail heard the slam of a door, and wondered if she'd be better off in Boston, married to James. There, she didn't have to learn "chores". Servants performed all the work. All she had to do was dress properly, meet his business associates, and bear James's children. *How hard is that?*

She recalled Mitch saying he'd help her to leave if it didn't work out. *It's not going to. I can't live amid all this anger and rude behavior. I have money, I can get a train ticket to just about anywhere.*

"Abigail?"

She turned her head to see Maryanne in the doorway. "Good morning."

Maryanne sat on the edge of her bed. "Apologizing for him is becoming a habit," she murmured. "I'm tired of it. Just understand we, Mitch, Gillian, and I, don't feel the way Silas does. Will that help you, dear?"

"I don't know." Abigail stared at the window, the gray light outside. "I wanted a husband, a family. How can I abide such hatred? And for such a stupid reason?"

Maryanne sighed. "I wish I didn't agree with you, but I do. I'd not want to marry into hateful chaos."

Lifting her pillows, Abigail sat up, resting against the headboard. "Why is Silas like this?"

"If I knew I'd slap some sense into him," Maryanne replied. "I don't. Until his father died, he was kind, generous, a loving husband to Gillian. Now he's a stranger. He's always riding Mitch, demanding work that Mitch tries to accomplish. Gillian admits she's afraid of him sometimes, but don't mention I told you that. It'll embarrass her."

"I won't."

Maryanne gripped Abigail's hand. "Please don't hold Silas's attitude against Mitch. Or Gillian and I. I haven't seen Mitch this happy in a long time. He's smitten with you, dear."

That statement warmed Abigail through. "You think so?"

"I do. He hasn't wanted a wife, seemed content to be a bachelor. Now he's floating six inches off the ground. Because he's met you."

Abigail felt her face heat. "It's surely not me."

"It is." Maryanne beamed and patted her hand. "Look, Gillian is making breakfast. Come and eat. You've had a long hard trip, and you need food. You're much too skinny, dear."

Knowing she'd lost weight on the train ride, Abigail didn't argue. "If I decide to stay, I must learn to be a rancher's wife."

"That takes time." Maryanne stood. "First step – get dressed. Come to breakfast. After that, we'll talk about being a rancher's wife."

Determined to pull her own weight, Abigail set about learning to cook, to launder clothes, to clean the home, and to feed the animals when necessary. With Mitch and Silas gone through the day, she swiftly learned how much was expected of the women in the west.

And no servants to do the work for her.

With Gillian at her side, Abigail stared in dismay. "I'm to what?"

"Milk the cow. It's not as hard as you think."

Cats prowled around her feet as Abigail shuffled amid the nasty, foul-smelling straw toward the huge black and white cow. The beast gazed at her with mild brown eyes, its jaws moving rhythmically. The calf bucked and kicked playfully, but Abigail found no amusement in its antics.

Terror seized her soul.

"Just watch me this time," Gillian said, sitting on a three-legged stool next to the beast. "You can't see anything from there. Come here."

Abigail edged toward Gillian, keeping the woman between herself and the cow that seemed to gaze into her soul.

"It's like this."

With the expertise of long habit, Gillian worked the cow's teats, squirting milk into the bucket. When the cow munched her hay with no concern at all, Abigail grew more confident.

"May I try?"

"Certainly."

Gillian vacated the stool, allowing Abigail to sit. "Don't jerk," she advised, standing at Abigail's shoulder. "Just pull gently."

Abigail pulled. The cow turned her head toward her as though wondering what she intended to do. Flushing, she tried again. The cow swished her tail into Abigail's face in irritation.

"It's all right," Gillian said, her hands over Abigail's. "Like this. Start slow."

Within minutes, Abigail caught the rhythm. She used her fingers to strip the teats, milk squirting into the bucket. She laughed in sheer joy, delighting in her accomplishment.

"I'm doing it!"

"Yes, you are," Gillian exclaimed. "See? It's all in the technique."

"And the cow doesn't mind?"

"No. She has more milk than her calf can drink," Gillian explained. "If we didn't milk her, her udder will soon grow too large and painful. And we share the bounty with the felines."

Abigail eyed the mewing cats roaming around with their tails high. "I don't know anything about cats."

"They kill mice and rats in the barn, and we give them some milk as a way of saying thank you. Without them the rodents would eat everything from the grain to our food stored in the cellar."

"Thank you." Abigail poured milk into a flat pan for the hungry cats.

Fascinated, she watched them lap the milk. "People in Boston keep cats as pets. My father forbade having any animal in the house."

"I had a pet cat when I was a child," Gillian commented. "I loved her. She slept in the bed with me."

Abigail stared in horror. "But the fleas. The filth."

"I bathed her regularly," Gillian answered calmly. "She was the furthest from filthy."

Abashed, Abigail glanced away. "I apologize."

"That's all right. You didn't know."

Gillian showed her the grain barrel, how to feed the chickens, and where the hens liked to hide their eggs. Trying to not think about the nastiness of reaching under a squawking hen to take the egg, Abigail fully realized just where her food came from.

"Do you butcher animals?" she asked, eyeing the pigs in their pen, snorting as they ate from their trough.

"Yes, and we grow vegetables in the garden."

Setting the milk and eggs aside, Gillian showed her the vast garden behind the barn, now barren for the winter. "We can most everything, then store them in the root cellar," she explained. "Down there, the food is safe from critters, and the cold as well as the summer's heat."

"You must show me."

They walked to the smokehouse as Gillian explained the smoking process. Abigail gazed at the shanks of pork, beef, and venison hanging on hooks, and considered how easily one might starve without the resources these people had. And how fortunate she'd been to grow up with enough wealth that finding, and storing, food wasn't a necessity.

"We have to store enough to get us through winter," Gillian went on. "Silas and Mitch hunt, which brings us fresh meat. Even without it, we raise the chickens, pigs, and cattle, of course, for food."

"And the ranch sells cattle to markets," Abigail mused, "and people in the east, like Boston, benefit from ranches like this one."

"Exactly."

Talking of Boston, and life on a working ranch, Abigail and Gillian fetched the milk and eggs, then returned to the house. Maryanne, at the kitchen counter making corn bread, glanced up as they entered. They removed their coats to hang on pegs, setting the milk and eggs on the table.

"You two were gone a while."

"I milked the cow," Abigail said with some pride. "My very first time."

"You're settling in very well then," Maryanne answered. "I'm very glad to see it."

"May I help you with that?"

"Certainly."

The day passed pleasantly as Abigail grew more comfortable with Maryanne and Gillian, and learning to cook. She'd been taught some basic cooking skills as a child, but as Abigail was intended to marry well, she'd rely on servants to do the household cooking and cleaning.

"You learn fast," Gillian commented as Abigail beat eggs and sugar together to make a glaze for the pie crust.

"I've good teachers."

When the three took a few moments to sit and drink hot tea at the table, Maryanne gazed at Abigail thoughtfully. "Can you be happy here, Abigail? I understand our way of life is so very different that what you knew back home."

"I don't know," Abigail replied slowly. "I'm used to servants. I was expected to marry a wealthy man where my only duties were to give him children and stand beside him at social functions."

"Why would you give that up to come here?" Gillian asked.

"I hadn't much choice." Abigail smiled sadly, thinking of Lily and her home in Boston. "My father ordered me to marry his business partner. A man I couldn't stand, and who'd make me very unhappy. I became a Mail Order Bride to escape a terrible fate."

"He was that bad?' Maryanne inquired, her brows up.

"Much worse."

"Then you did right by leaving," Gillian stated, patting her hand. "Mitch is the kindest of souls, and so very handsome. He's better looking than Silas."

Abigail burst into giggles, followed by Maryanne and Gillian. "Don't tell him I said that," Gillian added, laughing.

Amidst their amusement, Mitch burst into the kitchen in a flurry of bitter cold and snow on his shoulders. He carried in an armload of wood, using his foot to shut the door against wind.

"Snow coming," he said, his teeth chattering. "Might get bad."

"Where's Silas?" Maryanne asked, standing to help him stack the wood beside the stove.

"On his way," Mitch answered. "I saw him on the hills."

Abigail sighed inwardly, wondering if she looked forward to yet another evening of bitter sarcasm and back biting. Bracing herself for the attacks to come, she stood near the window, gazing into the yard.

"There's a horse and buggy out there."

Maryanne and Mitch exchanged a confused glance before striding to stand beside her.

"That's Hank Brown," Mitch said, a slight edge to his voice. "With Rachel."

He frowned at Maryanne. "Did you invite them, Ma?"

"No, I haven't spoken to them in ages."

Abigail caught the looks of alarm Mitch and Maryanne exchanged before Mitch went to the door and opened it. Unsure of what to do under these circumstances, Abigail joined Mitch, Maryanne and Gillian on the porch to receive their unexpected guests. Snow drifted down in large flakes even as dusk crept across the yard.

The aged man in the buggy, holding the horse's reins, waved at them cheerily. "Hi there, folks. Silas invited us to supper."

CHAPTER 6

Mitch ground his teeth in anger, but politely smiled at their unexpected guests. "Hello, Hank. Rachel."

"Come in out of the cold," Maryanne insisted. "Mitch, see to their horse, please. Poor beast shouldn't stand hitched in the storm."

"Sure."

He stepped from the porch to shake the old man's hand, offered a reserved smile to Rachel. Rachel, a plump, sort of pretty girl with black hair and beady brown eyes, simpered as he took her fingers to squeeze then immediately drop.

"Hello, Mitch. So good to see you again."

Shutting his teeth, Mitch nodded, then seized the gelding's bridle. Leaving his mother to make introductions, he took the horse to the barn. Fuming as he unhitched the horse from the buggy, he suspected Silas had invited them for the sole purpose of forcing a wedge between Mitch and Abigail.

"I'll kill him for this," he muttered, hanging the harness on the wall.

Outside the barn, the snow had thickened, the darkness deepening. He suspected Silas would wait until Mitch had completed chores, and when everyone had gathered in the house, he'd make his appearance. *Then I can't accuse him of plotting to ruin my fiancé's life. Not in front of guests.*

Without seeing Silas return, Mitch stalked to the house, brushing the snow from his coat. He absently thought that if the snow worsened, Hank and Rachel might be forced to stay the night. "I'll bet Silas planned that, too."

Stepping inside the kitchen, the tension came at him like a physical blow. He carefully glanced around as he removed his hat and coat, eyeing the polite smiles plastered on every face. Yet, behind hers, Rachel's dark eyes flashed hatred toward Abigail. Behind Abigail's lay insecurity, fear and hopelessness.

Maryanne and Gillian concealed their anger behind mild politeness and neutral faces.

"Come in, Mitch, you're late," Maryanne ordered, her tone harsher than Mitch was used to hearing.

Old Hank sat at the table, confusion clear on his craggy features. "Where's Silas, Mitch?"

"I'm sure he'll be here in a few minutes," Mitch answered, washing his hands.

Turning, he caught sight of Abigail's tight and miserable expression, and yearned to take her into his arms and comfort her. Rachel eyed her back with open hostility, only rearranging her face into a feigned smile when Maryanne gave her a stern look.

"What's this about you marrying this gal from Boston, boy?" Hank demanded. "Silas done told me you hankered to marry my Rachel."

Gritting his teeth, Mitch replied, "Silas should never have spoken for me. I'm sorry to be blunt, but there it is."

Rachel broke into a sharp sob, one Mitch knew to be fake. "I thought you wanted to marry me, Mitch," she wailed. "I want to be your wife."

At that moment, Silas entered the kitchen and the drama. As Mitch had, he took in the faces, Rachel's tears, his own expression set and closed. "Ah, you made it, Hank," he said, expansive. "I worried the weather would stop you."

"Nah, boy, a little snow won't hurt. Now look, Rachel's crying cuz Mitch has himself another gal."

"I wouldn't worry about that, Hank," Silas said, jovial. "Abby here will find life in Missouri too harsh. Right, Abby? You'll be heading home to Boston on the train real soon."

Abigail lifted her chin, green fire blazing in her eyes. "I'm adapting just fine, Silas. Thank you for worrying about me."

Caught between rage and laughter, Mitch choked for a moment. "Abigail is a tough woman. As tough as they come. Silas here already has a fine lady as his wife. He's just so used to Gillian's fine qualities he can't see it in other women."

Both Silas and Rachel instantly scowled.

"Everyone sit down," Maryanne ordered. "The stew's about ready. And we'll have a change of conversation as we eat. Right, Silas?"

Sullen, Silas sat next to Hank. "Yes, ma'am."

Mitch made certain to sit beside Abigail, making sure she saw his confident smile, his wink. His spirits rose a fraction upon seeing her tiny returning smile. In passing her the warm bread, he lightly caressed her fingers, and observed her faint pink blush.

"Y'all been losing calves to varmints?" Hank asked, his mouth full. "I done lost two to wolves."

"No," Mitch answered. "We haven't lost any. Have we, brother?"

Still sullen, Silas refused to answer.

"I'm gonna ride out and shoot them varmints," Hank grumbled. "Hang their hides on my wall. Can't afford to feed the wild critters. Shouldn't have to."

As Hank rambled on about his cattle, his land, and his problems, Mitch ate his stew with real hunger, absently thinking of Silas and Rachel. *What is going on? Something is. They're both in cahoots, planning my marriage. But why?*

It made no sense to him. Married to Gillian, Silas wouldn't have an affair with Rachel. Not if he's determined to get Mitch to marry Rachel. The more he thought about it, the less sense it all made. Silas's attempt to embarrass Abigail into fleeing the household obviously backfired. Badly.

As Gillian poured coffee, Maryanne peered through the cracked kitchen door. Even through the narrow space, snow blew in with a gust of icy wind. "You two must stay here tonight," she announced. "You can't go home in this."

"Aw, you can't put us up, Miz Ellison," Hank protested. "We can get home just fine."

"No, Hank, Ma's right," Silas said for the first time since dinner began. "You're not risking your lives just to go home. It's bad out there."

Rachel's expression appeared as though she'd bitten something sour. "I want to go home."

"No, honey," Maryanne assured her. "The storm is too fierce. You'll take the guest room and Abigail will sleep with me.

Mitch, you don't mind sleeping on the sofa by the fire? Let Hank have your room?"

Mitch plastered a smile on his face. "Warmest place in the house is on that sofa."

"Well, thank you folks," Hank said with a nod. "Grateful to you. My horse is fine?"

"In a stall in the barn with hay and water," Mitch answered.

"Good, good."

Hours later, the house silent, Mitch, wrapped in a thick wool blanket, tossed, and turned on the lumpy sofa. He considered leaving it to lie on the sheepskin rug on the hearth when the subtle rustling of clothes and the faint light from a candle glowed behind his closed eyes. He sat up and swallowed hard.

Garbed in Gillian's dressing gown, Rachel approached his makeshift bed. Her dark hair, unbound, trailed down her shoulders. "Mitch?"

"Yeah. I'm awake."

Rachel set the candle on the table. "Can we talk?"

"What about?"

"Us."

She sat gingerly on the sofa near him, not too close, but closer than he wanted her. Her pretty plump face was illuminated in red and gold from the fire and made her almost beautiful. In a very odd pose, she squared her shoulders, thrusting her chest toward him.

Mitch cleared his throat, uneasy. "Us? We're neighbors, Rachel. Your pa is our friend. There's nothing else between us."

She pouted, clearly aiming to appear seductive. "But we can be so much more, can't we? I believe we're meant to be together, Mitch. Man and wife."

"Silas put that notion in your head."

"No, no, he didn't. I've always admired you." She smiled. "The handsomest man in Culver's Creek."

"Well, I appreciate the compliment, but I've already asked Abigail to marry me."

The pout returned. "Silas says she'll not last another week here. Too soft for this country, he says. She had money and servants. I wish I had money for servants."

"Rachel, look," Mitch said, vying for patience. "I'm tired, it's late. Go back to bed."

"So, you're saying you won't marry me?"

"Yes. I'm saying that. Abigail will be my wife."

Rachel stood, closing the dressing gown with a gesture of finality. Her face tight with fury, she snapped, "Silas told me you wanted to marry me. You can't do this. If you don't marry me, you'll regret it."

Spinning, she stomped her way back down the hall and into the guest room. Too weary for such drama late at night, Mitch blew out the candle. After adding more wood to the hearth fire, he lay down on the rug, the blanket tucked around him. Wishing the uneasiness Rachel's words brought would leave him alone, he tossed about until he felt reasonably comfortable.

Still, sleep escaped him.

By morning, two inches of snow had fallen. Hank waved away Maryanne's insistence that he and Rachel stay for a while longer, declaring, "I got to care for my own stock, ma'am, and thank you. That itty bit of snow can't keep me from my place. We'll be fine."

Over breakfast, Mitch observed Rachel carefully not looking at him, and Abigail too busy cooking and serving to eat. Silas glowered into his bacon while Gillian patted his arm in her attempt to show him her love. Clearly trying to dispel the tension, Maryanne chattered away about the deep snow, the storm, and how much the land needed the moisture.

"Why, our rivers and lakes will be plum full by spring," she exclaimed, then tittered.

"Yep, that'll be right handy next summer," Hank agreed.

It was Silas who left the table without speaking, donning his hat and coat. A short while later, he drove the buggy to the veranda, and assisted Rachel up to the seat as Hank offered his thanks for Maryanne's hospitality. Hank also shook Mitch's hand.

"Think twice before marrying that Boston gal," he said, glancing sidelong at Abigail. "She'll bring you nothing but trouble, son."

Before Mitch answered, Hank clumped his way down the steps and into the buggy. As he picked up his reins, nodding to all who watched, he turned the horse.

Mitch knew he wasn't the only one who saw the expression of pure venom Rachel directed at Abigail before Hank snapped the reins on the horse's hindquarters. Despite the snow, the buggy had little difficulty in traversing the yard to the road before vanishing.

"Did you see that?" Maryanne murmured, awed. "The nerve of that girl."

"This is not right," Gillian snapped. "Who is she to get so uptight about Abigail being here? Silas, what are you up to?"

Only Mitch had noticed that Silas had gone straight into the house after seeing Rachel into the buggy. His thoughts from the previous evening returned to him, along with all the questions he had no answer for. As Maryanne and Gillian snipped and snapped over both Silas's and Rachel's terrible behavior, he watched Abigail go into the house.

He followed on her heels.

Abigail rushed down the hall to the guest room and tried to slam the door. Mitch's hand caught it before she could.

"Abigail, what's wrong?"

Her face crumpled as though she was on the verge of tears, yet her voice sounded hard, firm. "I'm leaving. I'm going home. I'd appreciate a ride into town."

Stunned, Mitch tried to take her hand, but she jerked away, and turned her back. "No."

"You said you'd help me leave if it wasn't working out," Abigail snapped. "It's not. I wish to leave. Now, Mitch."

He gently closed the door behind him. "No."

A choked sound emerged from her throat even as her shoulders rounded, her head bowed. "You can't keep me here."

Sliding his arms around her from behind, Mitch tucked her close to his chest. "Give me more time," he murmured into her hair. "Please. A little more time."

"You have something going on with that tart."

Mitch turned Abigail to face him. He cupped her pale cheeks in his palms and smiled into her damp green eyes. "I don't. Had I wanted to marry that tart, I'd never have placed that advert. You and I would never have met. Please. Stay. I haven't changed my mind that I want to marry you."

Abigail's lips parted. "You mean that?"

"Let me show you how much I mean it."

Pulling her closer, Mitch bent his face to hers, and kissed her.

CHAPTER 7

Bolstered by the revelation that Mitch wanted to marry her, Abigail went about learning her duties with a fervor. She attacked the house cleaning like a soldier going into battle, swept snow from the veranda, stripped linens from the beds for washing. Mitch tried to tell her to slow down, but Abigail ignored him. Silas made a few sniping comments before Maryanne shut him down.

"If you've got nothing pleasant to say, then keep your mouth shut," Maryanne snapped. "Now go outside and chop firewood. Maybe that'll calm your temper."

In the pantry, Abigail scrubbed the linens against the washboard, aware of the anger Silas directed her way even if he said nothing. He left the house on a wash of icy air, slamming the door behind him. Within minutes, the sound of an axe striking wood drifted to her hearing.

"I'm so sorry he's treating you this way," Gillian said quietly, joining Abigail. "I honestly don't understand why. He's normally so kind, considerate."

"He's simply taken a dislike to me," Abigail replied, not looking up from her scrubbing. "I told Mitch I want to leave. Go home."

"Oh, no." Gillian stopped Abigail with a hand on her shoulder. "Please don't leave us. Mitch would be devastated. As would Maryanne and me."

"He said he still wants to marry me." Abigail sighed, stretched her aching back. "That's helped me tremendously. But how do I deal with Rachel claiming she's the one who'll wed him? You saw the look she sent me."

"You don't deal with her," Gillian replied firmly. "We will. If she becomes a problem, which I'm sure she won't, we'll take care of her."

"And Silas?"

Gillian shook her head in regret. "Hope and pray he comes around. Ceases his silly animosity. Right now, that's all we can do."

"I appreciate your kindness, I truly do. If things don't improve, well, I'll have to consider returning to Boston."

"But your father will force you to marry that horrible man."

"By now, he's likely given up looking for me." Abigail smiled faintly. "Boston's a big place. I'll stay with Lily and her family until such time as I find a husband."

"Please realize we've come to love you. Mitch has grown so attached. He's so happy since you've arrived. You two are suited for one another."

"And I'm becoming attached to him," Abigail said quietly. "He kissed me last night. I've never been in love before. But I think I'm falling hard for Mitch."

Smiling broadly, Gillian took both of Abigail's hands. "That makes me so happy to hear. Somehow, we'll get things straightened out. Silas will come around."

"What if he doesn't?"

"He will. If he knows what's good for him."

"Have I told you how beautiful you are?"

Abigail felt her face heat in a furious blush. "Now that you mention it, no."

Maryanne and Gillian sat in the front room by the hearth fire, sewing as Abigail swept the kitchen floor. Mitch, having discovered her alone, grinned and slid his arms around her from behind. She shivered in happy delight as he kissed her neck.

"You're the most beautiful woman I'd ever seen," he murmured against her skin.

"And how many women have you seen in this tiny, remote place in a part of the country where you have so few women to choose from?" she asked playfully.

"Enough," Mitch replied. "I've been to St. Louis, you know. Big city."

Abigail offered a tiny snort and turned in his arms. "I came through St. Louis. It's not even the quarter size of Boston."

He lowered his mouth to hers in a long, slow, lovely kiss. "Then maybe you'll show me Boston one day. So I can see for myself the countless numbers of beautiful women."

"Perhaps I will. I do believe it may overwhelm you, however."

"Bah. No city in the world can overwhelm me."

"We'll see about that."

Loving the feel of his arms around her waist, Abigail was captured, unable to look away, from the warm affection she saw in his piercing blue eyes. His bright and happy smile, the attraction she sensed from him, and feeling her own for Mitch.

"You want children, yes?" he murmured.

"Of course. I adore children."

"How many?" he teased.

"At least three," Abigail replied with a light laugh. "Boys and girls."

"We should have three boys and three girls," Mitch speculated with a grin. "Keep it equal."

"You told me once that Gillian wants children."

"Oh, sure she does. She talks about it all the time."

"How can this house support that many children, Mitch?"

"We'll fix that by building our own house, darling. On the land we can call our own."

"Now that's a joke if ever I heard one."

Swiftly turning her head, Abigail saw Silas standing in the kitchen entryway, an evil smirk lurking about his mouth. Mitch instantly stiffened but refused to lower his arms from Abigail's waist. Glancing up, she watched his face darken with anger.

"Haven't you better things to do than eavesdrop on private conversations?" he growled.

"Nope. Not now."

Silas slid into a kitchen chair and leaned back, his smarmy grin not fading in the least. "You haven't told her, have you, little brother?"

"That's none of your business, Silas."

"It certainly is, since I'm the executor of Pa's will."

"What is he talking about?" Abigail demanded.

"Oh, Abby, you poor deluded child." Silas clicked his tongue, malice dancing in his eyes. "My brother here can't inherit the land he's talking to you about unless he marries. Pa's stipulation."

Abigail stared at Mitch, who flushed in growing rage, stepping away from her. "What does that mean?"

"He used you, Abby," Silas continued. "He agreed to marry Rachel, but to get back at me, he brought you here. He doesn't and never will love you or marry you."

Crossing her arms over her stomach, feeling sick, Abigail stepped away from Mitch. "Why are you saying this?"

"To tell you the truth, dear." Silas grinned but the smile didn't reach his eyes.

"That's enough," Mitch snarled, crossing the kitchen in long strides. "I'm done with your lies to Abigail."

Before Silas lifted his arms to defend himself, Mitch seized him by his coat and tossed him to the floor as easily as he might have thrown a chair. Silas crashed against the cabinets, rattling the dishes inside, momentarily stunned. Before he recovered, Mitch pounced, lifting him again and punched him hard across Silas's cheekbone and nose. Raising his hands, Silas offered a feeble resistance, aiming weak blows at Mitch's shoulders.

"What is going on?" Maryanne screamed, rushing into the kitchen with Gillian right behind her.

Ignoring her, Mitch struck Silas again, and released his coat at the same time. Silas reeled backward, blood flowing from his nose and mouth, and fell hard to the floor. As Mitch lunged, Maryanne charged into the fight and seized Mitch's arm.

"Stop it," she shrieked. "He's your brother."

"He's lying to Abigail," Mitch roared in reply, his blond hair failing over his eyes, his flesh dark with rage. "I won't have it, Ma. He's lying so Abigail will leave."

Gillian rushed past to kneel beside Silas as he struggled up, yet her face held little compassion or concern. "Why do you hate her so much?" she demanded. "You've no right to treat her this way. Mitch is right to beat you."

Pulling Mitch away from his prone brother, Maryanne planted herself between them. "Just what did he say?"

Mitch wiped sweat from his brow. "He told Abigail about Pa's will and stipulation. But he lied when he said I agreed to marry Rachel." He glowered down at Silas. "He lied when he claimed I brought Abigail here to get back at him. That I'm using her."

Maryanne stared fiercely at Abigail. "Abigail?"

"Yes," Abigail replied slowly. "That's what Silas said. If there is such a stipulation, then I cannot agree that Mitch is using me. If he must marry, then let him choose his bride."

Abigail met Mitch's hot blue eyes, her chin lifted. "You chose me."

"I did," Mitch replied. "I'm falling in love with you, too. And if Silas succeeds in forcing you to leave, I'll go with you to Boston. I won't lose you, Abigail."

"So be it."

With Gillian's help, Silas stood slowly, wiping blood from his nose and mouth. His upper lip curled. "You'll never make it in this country, Abby."

"That's not your decision," Abigail snapped. "Or your problem."

Maryanne turned. "I want to see the will, Silas. I'll read it for myself. Please bring it to me."

"I don't have it," Silas muttered. "It's in a box at the bank."

"Then you'll ride into town and fetch it." Maryanne advanced on Silas, forcing Gillian to step aside. "If you're trying to cheat

Mitch from his inheritance, I'll see to it you're removed from this ranch. I'll turn you out. Are you understanding me?"

Silas nodded, sullen. "Yes, ma'am."

"Your father would be so ashamed of you if he knew what you're doing to your own brother. I didn't raise you to be so cruel. Not to Mitch, and certainly not to his fiancé. Now clean yourself up."

His face lowered, Silas pushed past Maryanne and Mitch to exit the kitchen. Maryanne drew in a deep breath, glancing from Mitch to Abigail and finally to Gillian.

"Once again, I must apologize for what my son is doing to you, Abigail. Mitch, perhaps he'll settle down and accept things once you two are married."

Mitch crossed the floor to take Abigail's hand. "Would you care to move the wedding up? Say, in a week or so?"

A thrill of anticipation shot through Abigail. "Yes. I'd like that. You meant what you said about our own house?"

"I meant every word. I'll build you a nice, big house where we can raise our children. I'll have a real stake in this ranch, Abigail. I'll no longer be dependent upon Silas's generosity. Or lack of it."

"You shouldn't have to be now," Maryanne added with a sharp sniff. "I should have demanded a look at my husband's will a long time ago."

Craving his arms around her, Abigail slid her free arm around his muscled waist, her head on Mitch's broad chest. "I made the right choice, too."

"What do you mean?"

She gazed up at him. "Among all the letters asking me for my hand in marriage, yours stuck out as the best."

"Isn't that amazing?" Mitch held her close, chuckling.

"Don't forget the evil man she escaped from," Gillian commented. "Had you married him, you wouldn't have found Mitch. Or been as happy."

Mitch tilted his head back to look into her face. "You were engaged?"

"Not quite. My father demanded I marry his business partner." Abigail smiled, tracing her finger up and down his chest. "I put in the Mail Order Bride advert to escape them both. And I found you."

"I have to be the luckiest man alive," Mitch said with a chuckle, kissing her brow. "You chose me."

"I did indeed."

"All right, you two," Maryanne said, brisk. "It's time to begin supper. Mitch, see to your chores. Abigail, you and I and Gillian must begin making wedding plans. We don't have much time now, do we?"

Happy, overwhelmed by her growing love for her fiancé, Abigail smiled into his handsome face. "No, ma'am. We sure don't."

CHAPTER 8

"The sun is shining and the weather warm for once," Mitch said at breakfast two mornings later. "Care to take a ride in the buggy with me?"

Since their fight, Mitch hadn't seen much of Silas. He'd ride out just after dawn, and not return until well after dinner. He'd grab some cold roast, bread and fruit, take his meal to the room he and Gillian shared, then close the door behind him. Mitch knew both Maryanne and Gillian worried over Silas's behavior.

Until he gets his head right, there's nothing anyone can do.

Abigail glanced out the window. "That would be lovely. If Maryanne doesn't mind."

Deep in her thoughts and worries, Maryanne was startled out of her reverie at the sound of her name. "What? No, I don't mind. Girl, you've earned a break. You've been working so hard."

"We won't be gone but a few hours," Mitch added. "It gets cold early."

As part of her ranching education, Abigail accompanied him through the melting snow to the barn, watching as he showed her how to hitch a horse to a wagon or buggy. She asked intelligent questions, such as why the leather didn't create sores on the horse's body.

"We adjust all these buckles to make sure they fit properly," Mitch explained. "Too tight, the harness will rub sores. Too loose, and the whole thing won't work properly."

"The horse looks patient," Abigail observed.

"He's a good one," Mitch replied, stroking the gray's neck in affection. "Been our buggy and wagon horse for years. He knows his job."

"Does he enjoy it?"

"I'd like to think so."

Mitch helped her to sit in the high seat, tossed the bearskin in behind the seat. "In case the cold moves in quicker."

Seated beside her, Mitch clucked to the gray, setting him off at a brisk trot, hooves splashing through the muck. "I thought to take you on a tour of the ranch," he said.

"And the property you'll inherit?"

Mitch shrugged. "I'm not sure what part Pa left to me. We have a big spread. Nearly five thousand acres."

"How did your father get some much land?"

"My grandpa homesteaded it originally," Mitch replied. "He kept buying up property as it came up for sale. Same as what my pa did. Use whatever extra money they could to buy more land, borrowed money from the bank, bought more. Sold cattle year by year, paid the loans back."

"They sound like determined men," Abigail commented, gazing over the mix of forest and plains, now dormant for the winter.

"They were."

Following the muddy track that crossed the road that led into Culver's Creek, Mitch pointed out the ice-choked streams, the lazily grazing cattle. "Every fall we round up the two year olds and herd them to the market in St. Louis," he explained. "The cows are bred every year, raise the calves. Ranching sure isn't the easiest job in the world."

"Does the bad weather harm them?" Abigail asked, staring as the wide-eyed cows, calves at their sides, watched the buggy roll past.

"It can, if its bad enough," Mitch replied. "Cattle are tough. They know how to survive the winters."

Driving the gray gelding toward a certain area that offered a commanding view of western Missouri, and a stream rushing through it, Mitch urged the gelding up the steep climb. Abigail held onto the buggy's frame to maintain her balance as the buggy swayed back and forth. At the top, Mitch called, "Whoa," and halted the horse.

"I want you to see this," he said, jumping down, then striding past the patient gray to Abigail. "I think you'll appreciate it."

Her small hand in his, Mitch led her to the top of a steep cliff, the rushing stream forming a waterfall that dropped to the rocks and boulders below. All around, the landscape fell away in a breathtaking tableau of forests.

"This is incredible," Abigail exclaimed. "It's so beautiful."

"Yep. This is my favorite place." He turned them both and pointed. "See there? That flat area under those thick trees? That's where I always imagined building my house."

Abigail turned to him, her green eyes wide. "But can you? Will Silas permit it?"

Mitch shrugged. "Who knows? If he ever comes to his senses. The old Silas might have given it to me as a wedding present. What the new Silas will do? Make me buy it."

"That's not right." Abigail glowered. "You're brothers, for pity's sake. He has more than enough land that he can share with you. You work the ranch with him, yes?"

"I do, but he complains bitterly about what I do and when. Come on, let's walk around a bit."

As they walked, hand in hand, Mitch pointed out his dream home. "Build the house among the trees, they'll be protection from weather, the house will stay cool in summer. I'd put the barn over there, with sheds and a smokehouse between the house and barn."

"There's so much timber around here," Abigail commented.

"That and river rock." He gestured toward the stream. "Both make for a very solid house. I want to add a second story, a loft maybe, for the kids' rooms. A nice big hearth for cold winter nights."

He held Abigail close, absently wondering if he shared his hopes for nothing. That Silas would in the end refuse him any property at all, much less this gorgeous portion of the ranch.

"And we'd live in Maryanne's house while we built this one?" Abigail asked, her voice eager.

"Yep. That's the idea."

"I would adore living here," Abigail murmured.

Let's hope and pray we can. One day.

Mitch drove the gelding back down the hills, talking of the deer, the hawks, the bears, the wolves, the coyotes, and the badgers that shared the land with them. "The bears are hibernating now," he went on. "But come spring, they'll be out and hungry."

"Are they very dangerous?" Abigail asked.

"They can be. They avoid people and would rather leave when they see someone."

"I've never seen a bear," Abigail marveled. "Nor a deer, nor a wolf. There's a circus that comes to Boston with trained animals, but I've never been to it."

"Lions and tigers and all that?"

"Yes. My father always considered spending money on a circus was a waste of time. Thus, we never went."

"Your pa, he's a hard one?"

"I expect you can say that," Abigail admitted. "After my mother died, he passed me to nannies and housekeepers. He never hugged me, kissed me, or asked me about my day. In the end, I was merely a tool to advance his wealth and business."

"That sort of man doesn't deserve to be a father," Mitch rumbled, angry on her behalf. "Or be called a man."

"How would you treat your daughter?"

Mitch chuckled. "She'll be doted on, adored, given anything she wanted just short of spoiling her rotten."

"And your son?" Abigail inquired, smiling.

"The same. I'd teach him to ride, to hunt, to work cattle, to treat women like the queens they should be." Mitch smiled to himself, daydreaming of his son. "I'd teach him how to be a real man. To value the folks in his life, teach him honor and humility. Just as my pa taught me."

"Your father sounds like a wonderful man."

"He was. I sure miss him." Mitch grinned at her. "He'd sure approve of you joining the family."

"That's nice to know."

Mitch guided the gelding on, following another track to the north. "We've been out here for a few hours now, and we still haven't left our property."

"Where's the town?"

He pointed to the east. "That way. That road over there takes you straight in."

"There's so much to absorb," Abigail murmured. "I never thought there could be such beauty in the world."

"And Boston isn't beautiful?"

Abigail laughed. "I once thought so. Not anymore."

Following the road for a mile or so, Mitch gestured toward another track that led toward the west. "That takes you to the Brown place."

"Hank's ranch?"

"Yep. Starts right about here. You can see the roof of his house just over those trees."

Abigail lifted her head high to gaze in that direction. "Is that a rider on a horse?"

Mitch eyed the small moving speck. "Probably Hank out checking his cattle. He's got a small property, but it's rich in pastures and water. Awful pretty, too."

"It is lovely and gorgeous land. What are the summers here like?"

"Hot." Mitch grinned. "Humid."

"Not much different than Boston." Abigail sighed. "In the heat of high summer, the stink of the harbors makes life miserable. Of fish and rot. It's nasty."

"Out here, we smell the wildflowers and cow dung." Mitch laughed. "Can't be much worse than Boston."

"That sounds highly pleasurable. Without the dung, of course."

"I'm joking about the dung. Once it's dried, there's no smell at all. In summer, the flowers, the grass, and the trees all give off their own odors. Quite wonderful, I think."

The faint thudding of hooves caught Mitch's attention. Twisting around, he gazed past the buggy's frame to see the rider they'd noticed earlier. The horseman wore a big hat over his head, concealing his face, yet appeared smaller than Hank. He frowned, reining the gelding in, to watch as the rider cantered closer.

"That's not Hank," he said. "That's a gal."

"Rachel?"

"It would seem so. She seems bent on catching up."

He halted the gelding, then hopped down from the seat. Rachel, he knew, had never spent long hours in the saddle, disdaining riding over driving a buggy. She flopped loosely with every stride, her reins too tight, her heels clamped into the horse's ribs.

"Now what does she want?" he grumbled as Rachel rode closer.

"To apologize?" Abigail suggested, watching from the seat.

"Not likely."

Reaching him, Rachel yanked hard on the horse's reins, forcing its mouth open in protest. Mitch felt tempted to yell at her for her stupid cruelty, then simply seized the bridle. The horse chewed the bit in anxiety, its eyes rolling.

"What do you want, Rachel?" he asked, keeping his voice level, hiding his irritation.

"I saw you," she retorted. "You're trespassing."

"This is the public road," he growled. "Your pa's land stopped over yonder."

Rachel gazed past him to Abigail, her mouth twisting in hate, in rage. "Just ask me," Rachel snapped. "I'll say yes. I'll marry you. Get rid of her."

Mitch stifled his urge to swear at her, to turn the horse around and give it a good swat on the rump. "No."

"No? Ain't I good enough for you? I'm a far sight better than she is."

"Go home, Rachel," Mitch ordered. "And stop spreading lies. I never asked you to marry me."

"You did," she exclaimed, seizing the moment. "You don't remember, you were drunk, but you did. Just after your pa died. I remember."

"I was never drunk in your presence," Mitch gritted. "Now leave us alone."

"No." Rachel glared down, including Abigail in her hate. "You belong to me. Papa says so."

Turning his back, Mitch strode toward the buggy. "What your pa says doesn't mean anything. And you're as dumb as he is."

Before he reached the buggy, Rachel's shriek rose to break the tranquil quiet. "Dumb, am I? Dumb? I'll show you dumb! Hiyaaa!"

Mitch spun around at the sound of galloping hooves, seeing Rachel yank a pistol from under her coat. His eyes widened in horror as she bore down on him, aiming the gun at his chest. He froze for a moment, unable to think –

"Mitch!"

Abigail's scream hurtled him forward, across the horse's path. Lifting his arm, he caught Rachel across her belly, effectively rolling her out of the saddle and over the horse's rump. She landed in the mud with a distinct thud, and the gun went off.

The horse she rode and the placid gray both spooked.

The gray lunged forward at a gallop, taking Abigail and the buggy with him.

Mitch seized the saddled horse's reins a fraction before it bolted.

"Abigail!"

CHAPTER 9

Helpless, Abigail clung to the buggy's frame as it bounced, out of control, behind the galloping horse. She had no idea what to do. The reins flopped and flew somewhere in front of her, but she dared not leave her grip behind to grab them.

Do it. An inner voice ordered. *Grab them. You see them. Just pull.*

Fearing the buggy might overturn, dragged behind the panicked gelding, Abigail reached for the leather reins. Still, fearing to let go of her steadying grip, her fingers brushed the leather without enabling her to seize them.

The picture of the buggy crushing her body, ripping it apart as the horse dragged it, still at a full gallop, spun through her mind. *Do it. Or be killed.* Abigail let go of the frame.

She grabbed the reins in her left fist, then added her right.

"Whoa," she yelled, and hauled back as hard as she could.

The gelding replied.

He slowed to a canter, then a trot, down to a walk until he finally stopped still.

Shaking, Abigail clutched the reins in both hands, panting, terrified he'd panic again, race away despite her attempts to halt him.

Thudding hooves joined the thudding of her heart.

"Abigail," Mitch gasped, aboard the horse Rachel had ridden, reined in beside her. "Are you all right?"

Blinking, breathing hard, Abigail gazed at the now quiet gray, the serene fields, the birds flitting and chirping over the tall brown grass. "I – I think so."

"Whew." Mitch sucked in a deep breath. "You got him stopped."

Abigail gazed down at the reins in her hands, then at the now quiet gelding. "So I did." She laughed shakily. "I did. Didn't I?"

Mitch slid down from the saddle. "Come here. You need a hug. *I* need a hug."

He lifted her down, then pulled her into a tight embrace. Abigail, unable to halt her shaking, nearly wept from her terror. Her arms clasped around his waist, her face buried in his chest, she never felt so safe, and so loved, in her life.

"I'm proud of you," Mitch whispered. "You kept your head in a bad situation. No one can say you don't belong here in the west."

Calming herself, Abigail gazed into his blue eyes. "I love you, Mitch."

"How about that?" Mitch grinned, then kissed her. "The woman I love loves me back. Is that funny?"

Laughing away the last of her fear, Abigail finally remembered Rachel. She stepped a pace away, looking back the way they'd come. "Rachel?"

Mitch also glanced that way, his mouth a tight grim line. "She pulled a gun. Intended to shoot me, us. I reckon we'll let Freddie sort this out."

"Who's Freddie?"

"Fred Winston. The town's sheriff."

With Rachel tied to the saddle, shrieking her rage, Abigail sat beside Mitch in the buggy as he drove the placid gelding toward the town. With the coming of afternoon, the sun westered, and brought with it the predicted cold. Abigail huddled under the bearskin, listening to Rachel's unladylike curses.

"How does she know such language?"

Mitch chuckled. "Old Hank most likely."

"Maryanne and Gillian will worry about us."

"Nothing we can do about that now. Rachel must be turned over to Freddie."

At a building in Culver's Creek, Mitch halted the gelding in front, the sign overhead reading, *Sheriff's Office.* Tied to the buggy, the saddled horse also halted. Rachel, silent now but no less furious, shivered in the cold. Mitch helped Abigail down, still huddled under the bearskin, as a tall, young-looking man stepped from the office.

"Mitch," the sheriff said. "What are you doing with two gals? One of 'em Hank Brown's daughter?"

"I'll explain inside," Mitch said tersely, untying Rachel from the saddle horn.

In the warm office, Sheriff Freddie Winston listened as Mitch told of Abigail arriving as his bride, Rachel's insistence that Mitch marry her, her rage, and her attempt to shoot Mitch and perhaps also Abigail. Sitting beside the iron stove, Abigail drank hot coffee, listened, and watched Rachel's head fall lower and lower until it drooped onto her chest.

"Well, kids," Freddie said at last. "I reckon that's attempted murder. Twice over."

Rachel's head shot up, her expression stricken.

"But that's up to the circuit judge to decide," he went on. "I'll put her in a cell for tonight, feed her, let ole Hank know where she's at."

Mitch nodded, and gripped Abigail's hand. "Thanks, Freddie."

"This is your Mail Order Bride, eh?"

Abigail caught Freddie's admiring smile, recognized his warmth, his friendship. She smiled back, liking him through and through.

"I think you did good, Mitch," Freddie went on. "Glad you took my advice."

Abigail eyed Mitch, who shrugged with a grin.

"Freddie told me about the Mail Order Bride agency," he admitted. "I wrote that night. And so, we found each other, eh?"

She squeezed his fingers. "So, we did."

"Look, kids, as much as I like company, you'd best get on home. It'll be dark soon. If I know Maryanne, she'll be worrying."

"Yep. I'm sure she already is."

In the gathering dark and cold, Mitch helped Abigail into the buggy, wrapped the skin around her. He shook Freddie's hand, then climbed up.

"Say hello to yer ma," Freddie said, saluting.

"I will."

Abigail, huddling under the bearskin, leaned against Mitch for warmth, and thought about the rage that killed the soul.

"Thank God you're all right," Maryanne gasped, holding a lantern up as Mitch halted the now exhausted horse by the veranda. "Abigail, you look frozen through. Come down from there, right now. Let us get you into the house."

Stiff with cold and shaking, Abigail awkwardly climbed from the buggy and into Maryanne's and Gillian's arms. Mitch clucked to the gelding, turning the horse toward the barn as Abigail and her guardians helped her up the steps. The kitchen's solid heat hit her hard, yet she clutched the skin around her even as she sat in a chair.

"Gillian, hot tea, please," Maryanne ordered. "Don't talk, Abigail, we'll get your story soon enough. Just get warm."

By the time Mitch arrived after seeing to the horse, Abigail had dropped the skin, but continued to shiver. She drank the hot tea yet could not seem to get warm. His cold hands around his own hot tea, Mitch sipped and told their story of Rachel's attack. As he spoke, Abigail watched both Maryanne's and Gillian's faces tighten with anger.

"She'll have a piece of my mind," Gillian snapped. "How dare she try to shoot you."

"She'll spend time in jail, I guarantee it," Maryanne growled, pouring more tea into their cups. "Prison for years and years."

"No."

All eyes swiveled to Abigail.

"What?" Mitch asked.

"I don't want her in jail." Abigail firmed her resolve. "She's misguided and hurt. She'd been lied to. I'm sorry, Gillian, but somehow Silas lied to her."

Gillian nodded without speaking, staring into her cup. "I know."

"People do things when they're not thinking right," Abigail went on. "Sometimes bad things. Like today. Should Rachel carry that mistake for the rest of her life?"

"Yep," Mitch replied.

He smiled when Abigail caught his eyes. "But I'm willing to let it go," he added. "If that's what you want, my love."

"It is." Abigail swallowed. "My love."

Movement from the corner of her eye turned Abigail's face toward the kitchen doorway. Silas stood there, his gaze on hers, his expression neutral. A moment later, he turned, and vanished. Abigail suspected no one else knew he'd been there, listening. Nor would she say anything about it.

"Where's my Rachel?' Hank Brown demanded the following morning.

He'd barged into the kitchen without knocking, his face effused with anger and fear. "She went for a ride, never came back. Did you do something to her, boy? Did you?"

Mitch rose from the table to face the old man. "She's in town, Hank."

"In town?" Hank blustered, confused. "What's she doing in town?"

"She's in Freddie jail."

Hank's jaw dropped, showing his singular brown teeth. "Jail?"

"She tried to kill me, Hank," Mitch continued, his tone mild. "And Abigail. We took her in to Freddie. You can see her there, Hank. She's fine. She wasn't hurt."

Hank's seamed face closed. His narrowed eyes glittered. "This is your fault, boy," he growled, his finger tapping

Mitch's chest. "You led her on. Said you'd marry her. Then you find this Boston tart, throw my Rachel away. You'll regret this, boy. I'll see to it you do."

Hank stormed out into the dreary gray morning, mounted his horse, and rode away at a gallop. Abigail studied her meal, half-eaten, her appetite gone. How much of this was her fault? Did she do something to provoke this hatred? This level of violence?

Gillian gripped her hand. Abigail glanced up, surprised.

"I know what you're thinking," Gillian stated. "You think this is because of you."

"Well, isn't it?"

"No," Maryanne snapped as Mitch sat back down at the table. "Silas made claims he never should have. Why, I don't know. He wants Mitch to marry Rachel, and he encouraged a romance he had nothing to do with. That's not your fault. It's for Silas to acknowledge. Not you."

"Where is Silas?" Gillian asked. "He wasn't in our room when I woke up."

"Out riding," Mitch answered, his tone tired, weary. "He'll be in soon."

Except Silas didn't return home.

The sky darkened with ever thickening clouds, dusk arrived hours earlier than expected as Abigail looked out the window. Abigail eyed the growing darkness with worry, as Mitch had spoken of a possible blizzard on the way. She knew about blizzards and the white out conditions when one couldn't see feet in front of one's face. Where the wind howled around the eaves, and only fires in the stoves and hearths kept one from freezing to death.

Gillian paced the kitchen, frantic, near tears. "Where is he? Silas, come home. I'm so scared."

"He'll be here, Gillian," Maryanne assured her. "Be patient. Don't worry."

Outside, the rising wind screamed, and icy snow pellets battered the glass. Abigail's stomach roiled into a tight knot as she pictured Silas out in the madness of a winter's blizzard. *Come home, Silas. We're worried about you. Please be all right.*

Mitch burst into the kitchen in a wild hail of icy wind and snow. He put his shoulder to the door to shut it. Gasping, he tugged his hat off his head, and looked around with wide frightened eyes.

"His horse came back without him."

"Oh, God," Gillian screamed, collapsing to the floor. "Silas!"

Maryanne caught her on her way down. "We have to go find him."

Abigail seized her coat, her gloves, dragging them on as she spoke. "He can't be far," she exclaimed. "Right? He must have lost his way in the snow. We'll take lanterns."

"Right."

Grimly, Mitch lit spare lanterns and handed one to Abigail, and then to Maryanne. "If one of us finds him, we hang a lantern on the porch. Call in the others. Let's go."

Her blood rushing into her ears, Abigail burst into the blizzard, the icy cold blasting into her face. Struggling against the wind, she saw Mitch head toward the back of the house, Maryanne toward the barn. Of Gillian, she saw nothing. Clasping her coat around her neck, Abigail speculated that perhaps Silas had ridden toward town to see Rachel. And Hank.

Plowing through the rising drifts, the lantern held high and casting a faint illumination in a small circle around her, she struggled across the yard and toward the road.

"Silas!" she yelled, hoping he might hear her. "Silas!"

On and on she went, her hope sinking, dying. Silas could truly be anywhere. He may have fallen off his horse miles away and had already frozen to death in the storm. He may be buried mere yards from her, and she'd never see him.

Only her determination that Gillian not become a widow forced her onward.

"Silas!"

"Here."

His weak voice floated toward Abigail on the wind. Her light cast a faint shadow over his raised arm.

Gasping in disbelief that she's found him, Abigail knelt at his side. "Are you hurt?" she shouted to be heard over the howling wind.

"My leg."

Silas, his skin deathly pale, his eyes sunken into his cheeks, struggled to rise. "I can't walk."

"I'll help you. Put your arm over my shoulders. I've got you, Silas. I've got you."

CHAPTER 10

Mitch caught sight of the pale glow of a lantern. On the veranda.

He seized Maryanne's arm. "He's home! Come on, Ma, I'll help you."

Using the light as a guide, he half carried Maryanne toward the house. Stumbling, the wind all but blowing them over, they struggled and fought the drifts, the wind, and the deathly cold to slowly climb the steps. Mitch nearly slipped on the ice, almost taking Maryanne down with him, before regaining his footing.

He opened the door and pushed her inside.

Gasping, chilled to the bone, he pushed the door shut with his shoulder and latched it. Wiping snow from his eyes, he blinked.

Silas lay on the kitchen floor, covered in snow and ice, his face deathly white. Gillian knelt beside him, trying to unbutton his coat while weeping, her fingers shaking so hard she took several tries before managing even one. Also shaking from the cold, Abigail sat beside Silas, rubbing warmth into his hands.

Maryanne, dripping ice, opened the stove to add more wood. "He's too cold. We have to get his wet clothes from him before he freezes."

"Let me do that."

Mitch crouched beside Silas, unbuttoning his coat and lifting Silas so Abigail could pull it from him. Silas grimaced in pain at the movement, making Mitch wonder just where he hurt. "What happened, Silas?"

"My horse fell." Silas gasped as Mitch lowered him to the floor. "Rolled on me."

"Your ribs? Chest?"

"Mostly my leg."

Maryanne handed towels to both Mitch and Abigail. "Get him as dry as you can. Mitch, can you get him to his bed?"

"Sure."

As Gillian made hot tea, still crying, Mitch and Abigail dried Silas's hair and his damp clothes, bringing fresh circulation to his arms and legs. His cheeks turned from white to a dark red as he slowly warmed up. Mitch helped him to sit up to drink the tea.

"Put your arm over my shoulder," Mitch ordered. "I'll get you up."

Silas nodded, sliding his arm around Mitch. "Ready."

Abigail helped to boost Silas up and onto his good leg, then stepped back as Mitch and Silas made their way slowly from the warm kitchen. Mitch heard Maryanne order Gillian to cease her useless crying and to heat pans on the stove.

"I've got you," Mitch murmured, encouragingly.

"That's what she said."

Mitch eyed Silas in confusion. Silas managed a crooked smile.

"Abigail. She's one tough gal."

In Silas's room, Mitch helped him out of his still wet clothes and into bed. Covering his shivering brother, Mitch exposed only his injured leg. Turning black with severe bruising, Silas's leg began to swell. Sitting on the bed's edge, he glanced up as Maryanne entered.

She gazed at Silas's leg. "Is it broken?"

Mitch carefully probed, checking for breaks with his fingers as Silas groaned, writhing in pain. At last, Mitch shook his head.

"I don't think so. But he won't be walking for a while."

Gillian, her face red from crying, came in with two hot frying pans. Mitch stood by as Maryanne and Gillian put the warmers under the blankets to help Silas warm up. Silas accepted Maryanne's quick hug, then wrapped his arms around Gillian. He held her for a long time.

"Let's leave them alone," Mitch murmured, leading Maryanne from the room.

In the kitchen, Abigail had removed her coat, yet her hair and skirts were still damp. Busy wiping up the melted ice, she turned when Mitch and Maryanne entered.

"How is he?"

"He'll be fine." Mitch finally shed his own coat and dripping hat, then hugged her. "You saved his life."

"I was the one who found him. It could easily have been you."

"No." Mitch smiled, tucking a tendril of her hair behind her ears. "You were the one who guessed correctly. My focus was on the barn and that vicinity. I'd have searched there for far too long. You knew right where to go."

Abigail smiled, her arms around his neck. "I got lucky."

"How'd you get him to the house?"

"I just did. I had to."

"I love you, Abigail."

"Well, how about that." She grinned. "The man I love loves me back."

The blizzard blew itself out by the following morning yet left behind waist-high drifts and patches where the wind scoured the land clean. Mitch struggled to feed the stock, then waded through the snow to return to the house. After removing his hat, coat and boots, he accepted the hot coffee Abigail handed him.

"How's Silas?"

"Gillian says he's much better," she replied. "His leg pains him terribly, but he seems grateful he is alive. "The deep snow may have cushioned his body somewhat."

Maryanne stepped into the kitchen, her expression somber. "You're back. Silas wants to see you."

She motioned to Abigail. "Both of you."

Mitch exchanged a confused glance with Abigail but followed Maryanne down the hall and to Silas's open room. He lay with his back propped against the pillows, his face tight with pain yet looking far healthier than he had the previous night. Gillian sat in a chair at his bedside, holding his hand.

Abigail accepted another chair while Mitch and Maryanne stood. Silas nodded, his gaze flicking to Mitch and Abigail in turn.

"I have something that needs said," he began, his voice hoarse. "And offer my apologies. Whether you accept them is up to you."

Mitch rested his hands on Abigail's shoulders. "Apologize for the lies?"

"That and what I said about Pa's will."

"Go on."

Silas sucked in a deep breath. "There's no stipulation, Mitch. Pa left half the ranch to you. The northern half, including that spot you're so fond of. You didn't need to marry first. That demand came from me and me alone."

Mitch's jaw dropped. "And you couldn't tell me that last year?"

"Let's just say I felt you needed settling down." Silas tried a tiny smile, then it faded. "I wanted you to marry Rachel."

"That's obvious," Mitch snapped, holding onto his temper with an effort.

"Not for the reason you think." Silas glanced aside. "Hank promised to leave his entire property to us if you married Rachel."

"No," Maryanne gasped. "You lied and nearly drove Abigail away for the Brown place? That's despicable."

"Yes. It was despicable. His land is prime cattle property. Mitch would of course occupy it once Hank passed on. I did think Rachel would make him a good wife."

His gaze flicked to Abigail. "But Abigail makes a much finer mate for him."

Mitch took his hands from Abigail to avoid hurting her. He clenched his fists, grinding his teeth in rage. "Who are you to make my life's decisions for me? You're not Pa. You never had nor ever will have that right."

"I know. And I beg your forgiveness for trying."

Maryanne placed her hand on his arm. "Mitch," she said softly. "He did what he thought best for you, us. Even if his intentions were misguided."

"Misguided?" Mitch snorted, not placated in the least. "He tried to drive Abigail away with his lies, his torments. It nearly worked. Had he managed it, I'd have lost the best thing that ever happened to me."

"I thought Abigail wasn't worthy of you," Silas admitted. "Now I have to wonder if you're worthy of her."

His gaze rested on Abigail, who sat without moving. "As I lay in that snow, knowing I'd die, I thought of you, Abigail. And how I craved the chance to apologize before I passed on. I heard you say you wanted Rachel to never suffer for what she did. I must admit I never expected her to try to kill. But when she did, and you asked for mercy on her behalf, I knew then how I'd misjudged you."

"Thank you," Abigail murmured.

"I know it's probably too late," Silas went on. "But I hope you'll forgive me as well. And in time, maybe, we can be friends."

Rising, Abigail crossed the room to his side, and bent to kiss his cheek. "I think we're well on our way, Silas."

Angry, trying to find compassion and understanding, Mitch folded his arms over his chest. He studied the floor. "It may be a while before I can forgive you, brother. Not for what you've done to me, but what you did to her. And Rachel. She didn't deserve the lies, your deceit for land we could honestly purchase once Hank is gone."

"I've spent the entire night thinking that. And you're correct."

Abigail returned to Mitch, and slid her arm around his waist, snuggling against him. "I think we should postpone the wedding."

Mitch scowled. "Why?"

"Silas will be bedridden for quite some time." She smiled and Mitch lost himself in it, and her brilliant green eyes. "I want him to attend, Mitch. And, if she'll accept, I'd like Gillian to be my matron of honor."

"Oh, yes," Gillian cried. "You know I'll stand up with you."

"Thank you, Abigail," Silas said quietly. "That's the best gift you could possibly give me. I'm honored."

Mitch squeezed Abigail close. "Then we'll postpone. My wedding wouldn't be complete without my brother. Will you stand for me, Silas?"

Silas grinned. "I dared not hope for such, Mitch. I will. With pleasure."

Maryanne, tears streaming despite her smile, embraced both Mitch and Abigail. "Now my family is complete. Welcome, Abigail, to the Ellison family."

EPILOGUE

While Abigail hoped for sunshine on her wedding day, such was not to be. Clouds rolled in, threatening snow, as the pastor blessed their union in the Culver's Creek church. The guests numbered only twenty people, including Sheriff Freddie Winston. As Abigail and Mitch walked down the aisle amid thrown rice and shouts of blessings, she saw him beaming widely.

Freddie shook Mitch's hand, kissed Abigail's cheek as some guests streamed from the church. "You make the loveliest of couples," he said. "Many blessings on you both. Where will you be living?"

"We'll start building our home come spring," Mitch commented, holding Abigail's hand. "And we both hope you'll be a frequent visitor."

"You can't keep me away." Freddie cleared his throat. "I thought you'd want to know. The judge listened to you, Abigail, and is letting Rachel Brown go with a stern warning. Hank picked her up from my cell two days past."

"That's wonderful," Abigail exclaimed. "She doesn't belong in jail."

"From our conversations," Freddie went on, "she's learned her lesson. She's very sorry for what she did, and she'll probably come around to your place to tell you herself. And I made sure she knew you planted the bug in His Honor's ear."

"You didn't have to do that."

"I did it anyway. You'll just have to live with that."

"And Hank?" Mitch asked. "Is he still holding a grudge?"

"That I can't answer. He said nothing to me, just took Rachel home."

"He'll realize the truth," Maryanne said, approaching them. "He'll revert to being our friend and neighbor."

"Look," Freddie said, "you folks should be heading home. I think we have another doggone storm rolling in."

"Yes," Mitch said, glancing at Maryanne, with Silas and Gillian behind her. "Abigail and I are spending our wedding night in the hotel. But you three should get home."

"We will, brother." Silas shook Mitch's hand, kissed Abigail's cheek. "Congratulations, you two. We'll see you tomorrow."

Walking hand in hand with Mitch from the church to the hotel, Abigail wished Lily could have been there to see her married. "One day, we'll go to Boston. There are people I want you to meet."

"I'd love to meet them."

"Do you know how much I love you?" She gazed up into Mitch's smile, his warm blue eyes.

"Hopefully as much as I love you."

"More." Abigail smiled. "We're so blessed to have found one another."

Mitch bent to kiss her even as they walked down the sidewalk amid the rising, chilling wind. "And all because of two letters. How's that for our destiny?"

The End

CONTINUE READING...

Thank you for reading *Marrying Off His Brother!* Are you wondering **what to read next?** Why not read *The Bride's Surprise Visitor?* **Here's a peek for you:**

The first few days after her father's sudden death was the hardest time of Leila Anderson's life – or so she thought at the time.

Looking back, it was difficult to believe that the signs had been there all along, and yet she had not seen them. Her step-mother had never been an easy person to live with. Though Peter Anderson had loved her, somehow, she had driven him crazy with changeable moods and her unpredictable behavior. To her dying day, Leila was certain, she would always believe in her heart that Amelia Anderson's obsession with wealth and prosperity had contributed to Peter's heart condition and the attack that had eventually taken his life at the age of forty-seven. Even when she was small, even from the days shortly after Peter and Amelia were married, she could remember promising herself that if she ever found a husband, she would never treat him the way that Amelia Anderson treated her father.

Even her mourning seemed false. With great displays of weeping, she flung herself on the shoulders of every man who came within reach. Even Oliver Munson, the ancient solicitor for the Anderson family, was not exempt from her desire for consolation. But not consolation from just anyone, oh no – just the men, not any female friends or her own stepdaughter. When Leila had tried to put an arm around her at the funeral, Amelia had very firmly stepped away. As for others – well, Amelia Anderson had no female friends. Other women were useless at best, and competition at worst.

That had been just the few days after Peter's death.

It wasn't until afterwards that Leila began to understand just what she was in for.

Amelia Anderson had been solely focused on herself from the day she married Leila's father, and now that he was gone, she showed no signs of change.

"Leila, run me a bath. I have a headache."

"Leila, tell the cook to make me some broth, I feel a sickness coming on."

"Leila, if you can't make certain that the maid dusts the downstairs sitting room appropriately, then you must do it. I'm far too delicate of health to sit in all this dust."

Two days after Peter's burial in the little churchyard in Simes, Leila closed the door to his study quietly behind her. She took in a deep breath of the still, dry air and closed her eyes for a moment.

Visit HERE To Read More!

https://ticahousepublishing.com/mail-order-brides.html

THANKS FOR READING!

If you **love Mail Order Bride Romance, <u>Visit Here</u>**

https://wesrom.subscribemenow.com/

to find out about all <u>**New Susannah Calloway Romance Releases!**</u> **We will let you know as soon as they become available!**

If you enjoyed *Marrying Off His Brother,* would you kindly take a couple minutes to leave a positive review on Amazon? It only takes a moment, and positive reviews truly make a difference. Thank you so much! I appreciate it!

Turn the page to discover more Mail Order Bride Romances just for you!

MORE MAIL ORDER BRIDE ROMANCES FOR YOU!

We love clean, sweet, adventurous Mail Order Bride Romances and have a lovely library of Susannah Calloway titles just for you!

Box Sets — A Wonderful Bargain for You!

https://ticahousepublishing.com/bargains-mob-box-sets.html

Or enjoy Susannah's single titles. You're sure to find many favorites! (Remember all of them can be downloaded FREE with Kindle Unlimited!)

Sweet Mail Order Bride Romances!

https://ticahousepublishing.com/mail-order-brides.html

ABOUT THE AUTHOR

Susannah has always been intrigued with the Western movement - prairie days, mail-order brides, the gold rush, frontier life! As a writer, she's excited to combine her love of story with her love of all that is Western. Presently, Susannah lives in Wyoming with her hubby and their three amazing children.

www.ticahousepublishing.com
contact@ticahousepublishing.com

Made in the USA
Monee, IL
16 May 2023

33840779R10070